THE BODY IN THE PARK

A RAZZY CAT COZY MYSTERY #1

COURTNEY MCFARLIN

D1737716

D & K Books

For my sweetheart - your love and support make all of this possible.

CHAPTER 1

Friday, June 19th

*T*he hum of the newsroom refused to fade into the background as I worked to file my last story for the day. I'd been assigned a fluff piece, which I usually hated, but considering it was almost the weekend, I wouldn't complain too much. I was looking forward to two blissful days off and some quality time away from work.

I've been working at the paper here in Golden Hills, Colorado, for two years, ever since I graduated from the local college. I'm originally from a tiny town in South Dakota, and I love living so close to the mountains. I'd discovered a love of hiking while I was in college, and I couldn't imagine leaving to go back home to the family farm. There's nothing wrong with farming, we all gotta eat, but for me, I needed mountains and adventure.

I read through my story one more time, checking for errors, stopping to admire my byline. Hannah Murphy, that's me. Seeing my name in print never got old. I hit enter on my laptop, posting my story to my editor with plenty of time to spare on my deadline. I rummaged around under my desk, looking for my purse. With any luck, I'd be able to slip away a bit early and head home. I poked my head over my cubicle and looked over at the glass office where my editor, Tom Anderson, was banging away on his computer. I stifled a laugh. Tom was old school, from a time when the clerical girls typed everything on typewriters, and he resented being forced to use a computer.

I grabbed my things and headed down three cubicles to where my best friend, Ashley Wilson, worked. Ashley was my roommate in college, and we were both journalism majors. While she lived for the lifestyle pages, I was drawn to the hard news and wanted to make a name for myself as a reporter. I wasn't kidding myself. I knew it was a miracle our little newspaper had its doors open still. Most small newspapers had folded years ago, and it was tough for an independent outfit to keep the lights on. But I was hoping with some luck, perseverance, and hard work, I'd be able to move up the ranks to a serious news position.

I tapped on the wall of Ashley's cubicle and flopped into the chair across from her desk.

"Hey, Ash, you about done for the day?"

Her tongue was poking out from between her lips as she focused on her screen, ignoring me. I leaned over to see what was engrossing her and saw she was working on an image in Photoshop. Since we were such a small paper, most of us had to do our design work for our stories, which wasn't always fun.

I watched her as she worked, admiring her long brown hair that was impossibly straight and glossy. My hand went up to my unruly nest of blonde locks, and I gave a rueful smile. No matter how often I tried to straighten my hair, it never turned out as pretty as hers.

We were complete opposites. She was tall, statuesque, and dark, while I was short, thin, and fair. She enjoyed shopping and partying, while I was an outdoors kind of girl. It didn't matter, though. I'd never had a friend as close as her. She gave a little shout and hit save, turning to face me.

"Hey Hannah, sorry about that. The image didn't want to

2

cooperate."

"No worries, been there, done that. What are your plans for tonight? Are you hanging out with Bill, or was it Will?"

"Will. He was also three guys ago. You gotta keep up, girl!"

"Sorry, are you hanging out with what's his face tonight?"

"I was unless you wanted to do something. We need a girl's night out."

"We do, but not tonight. I think I've got a migraine coming on. I'll just go home and hang out with my cat."

Ashley made a sad face and heaved a sigh.

"That's how it starts. You're in your twenties, and you spend a Friday night alone, with just a cat for company. Before I know it, you'll be my crazy cat lady friend who becomes a shut-in and only leaves to buy more cat food."

"Wow, that's a depressing and strangely detailed future look."

"I call them as I see them. I kid, Hannah. You should get out more, though," Ashley said, giving me a look.

"I know, I'm just not a peopley person. I enjoy being outside, not cramped in a loud bar with sweaty people being all, I don't know, sweaty. I like my cat. I like quiet."

"I need to find you a man. I think Will had a brother..."

"Thanks, but no thanks. I don't want to get set-up with a cast-off's brother. That would be even sadder than being home alone with my cat. Seriously though, have fun tonight. I expect a play-by-play tomorrow."

Her phone rang, cutting off our conversation. I waved as I grabbed my bag to leave. It looked like the coast was clear, so I headed towards the door, determined to make a break for it. I wasn't lying to Ashley, my head was pounding, and I wanted to get home and change into my jammies.

"Hannah! Wait!"

I groaned when I heard Tom's voice, turning in my tracks to head back to his office. I stopped in the doorway.

"Hi, Tom. How was my article? Does it need any edits?"

"It was fine. You self-edit well. That's not why I wanted to talk to you," Tom said, gesturing for me to come in and take a seat.

I plopped in the comfy chair across from his desk.

"What's up?"

The way Tom dressed was as old school as the way he typed. His button-down shirt was turned up at the cuffs, exposing a myriad of ink stains. He had a nice face, utterly at odds with his gruff voice. He scrubbed his bald head and leaned back in his chair. He looked at me closely for a beat.

"Hannah, you've been doing a great job lately. I know fluff pieces aren't what you want to do, and I appreciate you've been good about working on them. I can tell you put the effort in, even though you don't enjoy the subject."

"Thanks, Tom, that's nice of you to say."

"I'd like to try you out on a few tougher pieces. The next big story that breaks is yours."

"Are you serious? I'd love to try some harder news pieces!"

This was the most exciting thing to happen to me in months. I was finally going to sink my teeth into some meaty stories!

"That and whatever else you can dig up. I know you're young, but I think you deserve a shot."

"Thank you so much. I won't let you down."

"See that you don't."

With that, he waved me off and turned back to his computer, cursing under his breath as he started banging on the keys again.

I floated out of his office, almost forgetting my headache. I got to the parking lot and climbed into my ancient Chevy Blazer. I'd saved up my money back in high school, and it was old back then. It'd seen me through college, though, and with any luck, it would get me through until I could make enough money to replace it.

Traffic was picking up as I navigated my way back to my apartment. Golden Hills was growing fast, but I was lucky enough to find a place that backed right onto a huge green space. I had acres and acres of wilderness to explore via the trail that led to the Crimson Corral park. It wasn't cheap, but it was worth it to have an outdoor space and a killer view.

I trudged up to the top floor, feeling my headache get worse with every step. By the time I made it to my door, I was feeling odd. I walked in and immediately tripped over my cat, Razzy. I'd had her for two years, ever since I got my place. I scooped her up and cuddled her close, apologizing for tripping over her. She was a Ragdoll cat, and I had no idea how a beautiful, purebred cat like her had ended up in an animal shelter.

Her soft fur felt like a rabbit, and her little purrs made me smile. She was a quiet cat who rarely meowed. I put her down and walked to the kitchen, trying to decide what to make for supper. A quick check of the fridge revealed I needed to do some serious grocery shopping. As I stood in front of my cabinets, a wave of nausea and dizziness rushed through my body. I gripped the counter to keep from falling over.

Razzy meowed at me, cocking her head to the side. It was like she could tell something was wrong. I skipped dinner and walked back to my bedroom, holding my head. I changed into my favorite pair of fuzzy pajama pants and a tank top. Maybe if I just lay down for a few minutes, I'd feel better. I collapsed onto the bed, and Razzy jumped up next to me, snuggling close. Closing my eyes, I felt darkness rush towards me.

* * *

"Mama? Mama!"

A small voice pulled me from the darkness. I blinked open my eyes, trying to get my bearings. I felt grass underneath my feet. I looked around and realized I was in a park. My stomach felt hollow as I looked around, trying to figure out why I was outside. I glanced down and saw I was still wearing my fuzzy pants and smiled. This must be a dream. At least, in my dream, I didn't have my headache.

"Mama?"

There was that voice again. I looked through the gloom, trying to see if a child was wandering around. This was a strange dream for sure.

"Mama! There you are."

A small figure walked towards me and sat in front of me, looking up into my face. It took me a second to recognize my cat, Razzy, sitting there. Her whiskers bristled in the faint light from the moon.

"Say something, Mama. You're scaring me. Why are you outside?"

I felt my world rock as I realized Razzy was talking to me. Like, really talking. I laughed when I remembered I was dreaming. Geez, this was one crazy dream. I shrugged and went with it.

"Razzy, what are you doing in my dream?"

"Um, I'm pretty sure you're not dreaming. I followed you out of the apartment. You left the door open, which isn't safe, by the way. I tracked you here and kept calling you until I found you. Why didn't you answer me?"

Ok, this was weird. She was talking to me like she was a human, and I could understand everything she was saying. This had to be the winner for my strangest dream ever.

"You were calling for mama. I figured there was a little kid in my dream who was looking for their mother. I didn't know it was you."

"I always call you that. To me, you are my mama," Razzy said, her eyes rounding with concern. "This is weird, though. I always try to talk to you, but it's like you can't understand me. Why are you suddenly understanding what I say?"

"Must be the dream. I'm sure I'm going to wake up any second and find you cuddled up next to me."

"You're not dreaming, but whatever. Can we go home now? It's getting cold."

Razzy fluffed up her fur and turned to her left, looking at me expectantly. Her tail curled into a question mark as I stood there, staring at her. Well, maybe if I followed her, I'd wake up. I must have had something bad for lunch.

I shrugged and followed her.

"Lead on, MacDuff," I said, as I fell in behind her.

"It's actually 'Lay on, MacDuff,'" Razzy said with a sniff. "Humans, always misquoting things."

"Wait, you know Shakespeare?"

"I know way more than you might think."

I couldn't help but laugh. I had a talking cat who was also a literary critic in this dream. I needed to write this down when I woke up.

Razzy paused, her tail going stiff and then curling down behind her. Her hackles went up, and she sniffed the air.

"Stop, there's something up ahead."

"Are we going to meet a talking dog next? That would be pretty cool."

I moved past her, ready to get out of this dream and wake up back in my apartment. I took a few more steps and fell over something stretched across the sidewalk. As I felt around to see what I'd tripped over, my hand came in contact with something cold and squishy. With a little shriek, I scooted back. This dream had taken a disturbing turn.

I felt in the pocket of my pajama pants and grabbed my cellphone. Switching on the flashlight app, I held it out in front of me, my hands shaking. I wasn't sure I wanted to see what it illuminated.

There, next to me on the ground, was the body of a man. I placed my fingers on his neck and felt nothing there. Jumping up, I screamed, convinced now was the perfect time for me to wake up. I looked over at Razzy. She walked closer, sat down, and shook her head.

"I told you, you're not dreaming. You should probably call the cops."

Realization flooded through me as I took stock of the situation. My feet were freezing on the cold concrete. I checked my arms and noticed I had goosebumps. I pinched myself and winced when I clearly felt it.

Razzy walked over to my feet and gently bit down on the top of my foot.

"Ouch! Why did you do that?" I asked, rubbing my foot.

"You didn't seem to believe me you're awake. You were pinching yourself, so I thought it would help if I pitched in too." She gave what I assumed to be the cat version of a shrug. "Call the cops."

I hesitated for a second before numbly obeying her suggestion and punching 9-1-1 in on my phone.

CHAPTER 2

Saturday, June 20th

*A*s I waited for the police to arrive, I started pacing back and forth. I had the dispatcher on the line, but I wanted to talk to Razzy and figure out what the heck was going on. The temperature dropped a little, and I looked at the time on my phone. It was just after one in the morning. I couldn't believe this was happening. I went through everything I knew up to this point.

First, apparently, I was not dreaming. This was all too real. I glanced down at my pajama pants and winced. Why couldn't I have worn my regular black pants? These were bright pink and featured white cats all over them. I would be ready for the crazy cat lady of the year award at this rate.

Second, why could I hear Razzy talking? This was not normal. I mean, I was one of those cat owners who carried on conversations with her cat, but until an hour ago, they were all one-sided conversations. I think. Maybe she had been talking back, and I just never realized it.

Third, who the heck was the dead person on the sidewalk? I thought back to the minutes after I first woke up in the park. I'd heard Razzy calling for me, but nothing else. Did that mean the body was dumped before I reached the park? Had I been sleepwalking?

I groaned, frustrated at the thoughts rampaging through my head. The dispatcher on the line heard me and asked if I was ok.

"Yes, sorry, I was just thinking."

I gave up pacing and joined Razzy on the nearby park bench to wait for the cops.

"Now, that's sensible. There's no point in wasting all your energy," Razzy said, giving her flank a final lick.

I was going to answer and then remembered I was still on the phone.

"Miss, is there a cat there?" the dispatcher asked.

"You can hear her, too?"

"Well, I hear meowing, so yes, I heard what I assume to be a cat," she said.

"I mean, yes, there's a cat here. My cat came with me to the park."

I swear I could hear the dispatcher rolling her eyes through the phone. Great, just great. I'm now the crazy weird person who found a dead body in the park, in the middle of the night, with my cat in tow. This was going to be great for my reputation.

I heard sirens and looked up to see flashing lights as two cop cars pulled up.

"The cops are here. I'll let you go," I said, hanging up the phone. "Now, Razzy, be quiet. We don't want to look crazy."

"I never look crazy. But you..."

"Hush!"

"Miss, are you the one who called in a dead body?" the first cop asked.

"Yes, it's right over there."

I pointed down the sidewalk and wrapped my arms around my waist, trying to stay warm. The two cops went down the path, and I heard more sirens approaching. An ambulance pulled in, and there was a flurry of activity as the paramedics jumped out and grabbed a gurney. As I watched them run down the walk, another man approached me. He was dressed in a suit and looked official.

"Miss? I need to ask you some questions," he said as he approached.

As he got closer, I could make out his features. He had short sandy blonde hair. His eyes were startlingly light, but I couldn't make out the actual color. His face was chiseled, and if I hadn't just fallen over a dead person, I might have been attracted to him.

"Yes, I'll be happy to help," I said. "Who are you?"

"I'm Detective Ben Walsh, with the Hills police department. Can I get your name?"

"I'm Hannah Murphy. I'm a reporter with the Post."

"Oh, you're a reporter. I see."

I didn't miss the look of distaste he shot me. Ah, he was one of those cops who didn't like reporters. I heaved a little sigh.

"I'm a reporter, yes, but I'm a viable witness. I found the dead guy over there about half an hour ago."

He glanced at the cat sitting next to me and my pajama pants and quirked an eyebrow.

"Is this your cat?"

I cleared my throat, embarrassed to be caught in this situation.

"Yes, this is my cat, Razzy."

He held out his hands, knuckles first for her to sniff, before patting her on the head.

"Nice cat."

"Oh, he's cute," Razzy said. "Don't screw this up."

"What?" I asked.

"I said nice cat. Now, can you tell me what you're doing in the park this early in the morning?"

I needed to get a grip. I couldn't be answering my cat right in front of this guy. What was my problem? I put my head in my hands and tried to come up with a good reason for walking in the park in my pajamas with my cat. A reason that wouldn't implicate me in the death of whoever the corpse was.

"I had a bad headache earlier, and I thought maybe some night air would help," I said. "So, I took a walk. I live right over there. Some-times, my cat likes to come with me."

That felt pretty lame, but it was all I could come up with on short notice. What? I may be a reporter, but this situation was out of my wheelhouse.

"You took a walk. At night. Alone, with your cat?"

"Yep, we do that sometimes."

"Ok, did you hear anything before you discovered the body?"

"No, I was surprised when I fell over him. I honestly don't know who he is, or was, or why he's here."

I ran my hands up and down my arms to warm up. Ben must have noticed me and shrugged out of his suit coat, offering it to me.

"Here, you look cold. What time did you leave your apartment?"

I gratefully accepted the jacket and wrapped it around my shoul-ders. I couldn't help but notice it smelled like sandalwood. I sat for a moment, trying to think back to the timeline of when I'd woken up and when I'd fallen asleep. A lot could have happened in between, but I was only aware of the past hour.

"About an hour ago, I think. I found him about thirty minutes ago and called the police. That's all I know."

His eyes narrowed as he searched my face. I smiled up at him, hoping he wouldn't ask any more questions.

"Well, that's all I have for now. I'll need you to come down to the station later in the day to give your prints. Can you give me your address and contact information? I may have more questions for you later."

"Sure."

I rattled off my address and phone number and stood up. I was so ready to go home and go to sleep. Fatigue was sitting on my shoul-ders, making his coat feel like it weighed fifty pounds. Speaking of his coat, I slipped it off and handed it back to him.

"Thanks. I'll be in touch later in the day. If you think of anything else, here's my card. Now, I know you're a reporter, but I'm going to ask you to keep this quiet. I know your colleagues are going to be swarming here soon, but you obviously know more than they do. I don't want to see any of it in print."

My head snapped up.

"What do you mean, keep it quiet? I just found a dead body in the park next to my apartment. If that isn't news, I don't know what is."

He sighed and pinched the skin between his eyebrows.

"That came out wrong. I'm asking you not to give too many details in your story. I know you're going to write about it, your kind always does. This is an investigation, and we need to find out who's responsible. As of now, I only have one suspect," he said.

"Wait, my kind? What do you mean, my kind? And who's your suspect?"

"You're a reporter. Your kind always sticks their noses in where they don't belong and mucks up investigations. And if you've been a reporter for any length of time, you already know the person who finds the body is always the first suspect until more leads come in. Did you kill him?"

"What?"

My screech was so loud, Razzy sat bolt upright, fur standing on end.

"Mama, don't scream at the nice man. He's just pointing out the obvious. You know that."

"Keep quiet!"

"Excuse me?" Ben asked.

"Not you, the cat. I didn't kill the guy. If I had, why on earth would I be standing out here, freezing my tuchus off and waiting for the cops to arrive? If I killed someone, I wouldn't go to that kind of trouble."

Ben looked at me and took a step back, raising his hands.

"Ok, ok. Just come down to the station later and give me your prints, all right? When you file your story, stick to the bare facts. Let me know if you think of anything else that might be helpful."

He walked towards the uniformed officers and paramedics, dismissing me with a wave. Well, this morning was undoubtedly starting just peachy. I scooped Razzy up, cradling her to my chest to keep myself warm.

"Mama, you weren't very nice to the police officer."

"I know, but that was rude of him to say. Like I'm going to kill anyone."

"We both know that, but he's just doing his job. That's what the cops on the television always say."

"You can understand television?"

"I understand a lot. Now that we can communicate, I have questions for you, though. And I'm hungry. Can we eat something when we get home?"

My stomach grumbled, reminding me I'd skipped dinner.

"Yeah, let's have an early breakfast. I need to file my story as soon as I get home, and then we can eat."

Razzy gave a little sigh and swiped her raspy tongue over my chin.

"Thanks, mama."

Within a few minutes, we were back home. I walked through the open door into my apartment and froze. What if someone had come in while we were gone? I gently placed Razzy on the back of the couch and crept through down the hallway. A thump made me jump out of my skin until I realized Razzy had jumped down and followed me.

"What are you doing?"

"Seeing if anyone broke in while we were gone."

She chuckled and swiped a paw over her face.

"Silly, I could smell if someone had. We're alone. Now, you mentioned breakfast?"

I walked back to the kitchen in a daze as I tried to process everything. How on earth had this happened? I pulled a can of Razzy's food out of the cupboard and dished it up for her. I went to put it on the floor.

"Now that you can understand me, I much prefer eating at the table with you. It's more civilized," Razzy said, jumping up on a chair at the kitchen table. She looked at me expectantly.

I slid the dish onto the table in front of her and grabbed my laptop. Joining her at the table, I pulled up my paper's software portal and planned my story. The loud slurping noises from the end of the table distracted me. I paused and looked over at her.

"Could you keep it down a little?"

"Oh, sorry, it's just so good."

I went back to my thoughts and wrote up a short description of what I'd seen in the park. It wouldn't be much, but I should be early enough to make it in today's edition. I looked at the clock and saw it was a little after two. I grabbed my cellphone and paged through my contacts until I found Tom's entry. It took four rings for him to answer.

"Do you know what time it is?" Tom asked.

"It's time for a late-breaking murder story."

"What?"

"You're never going to believe this. I was walking in the park right near where I live, and I found a dead body."

"You didn't kill them, did you? I know I said you could have the next big story, but I didn't mean you had to go out and create it."

"Geez! Why does everyone keep asking me that? I'm like five one. I'm too short to murder anyone."

"Hey, crazier things have happened. Write up your story and get it submitted right away. I'll call the night desk and make sure it makes it to the front page."

"One step ahead of you. I just posted it on the portal."

"That stupid thing. Well, I guess the night desk can deal with it."

"I'll follow up with the story here in a few hours. I need to meet with the lead detective and give my prints. I'll see if we can get more details."

"Sounds good. Keep me posted. Later, though, I'm going back to bed."

Tom hung up the phone and I chuckled. His gruff demeanor couldn't fool me. Razzy's bowl made a clattering noise as she swiped her tongue around it, getting every morsel she could.

That reminded me I needed to eat something if there was any hope of me getting some sleep. I padded into the kitchen and searched through the freezer before finding an ancient frozen waffle. It would work, I guess. I brushed off the freezer crystals and stuck it in the toaster. A quick search of the cabinets revealed an old bottle of pancake syrup. I didn't think the stuff could go bad.

The toaster shot my waffle skyward, startling me again. I tossed it on a plate, burning my fingers, and doused it in syrup. Deciding to forgo my manners, I ate standing up, rinsing the dish off in the sink when I was done.

"Come on, Razzy, let's go to bed. Maybe this has all been a dream after all."

"You're not dreaming. Besides, I love that you can understand me now. I wouldn't want that to change."

She rubbed against my ankles and my heart twinged. If I was honest, I wouldn't want to wake up and find out it was a dream, even with all that had happened. I picked her up and held her close, walking back to my bedroom. She settled on the bed next to me, and her soft purrs lulled me to sleep.

CHAPTER 3

*I*t felt like I had just fallen asleep when I heard an annoying ringing noise coming from next to my bed. My sleep befuddled brain was trying to figure out what to do when I felt a soft paw on my shoulder.

"Could you shut that off, please?" Razzy asked, yawning widely.

"Gah!"

Razzy shot up on all four legs and looked around with wide eyes.

"What? What's wrong?"

"You're talking. It wasn't a dream. Oh my God, I can understand my cat."

"We went over this last night. Could you please answer that? It's annoying," Razzy said, flicking her tail and settling back down on the pillow.

I sat there for a second, trying to collect my marbles. I'm pretty sure a few of them might have escaped for good the night before. My phone stopped ringing as the call went to voicemail. Ok, so I could understand Razzy, which meant I wasn't dreaming the night before, which also meant I really did trip over a dead body.

If I was going to keep processing this, I was going to need a lot of caffeine. I grabbed my phone and hit the voicemail button as I went to the kitchen to make coffee. Ashley's voice shouted through my phone's speaker, making me wince. I slid the pot out of the machine and started filling it with water. As I waited, I glanced at the time on the stove. It was just after nine in the morning. I'd gotten a whopping four hours of sleep.

After I added some coffee grounds, I slapped the start button and leaned back against the counter, waiting for my life-giving brew to finish. I still couldn't believe what had happened. How on earth did this happen to me? I chewed on my thumbnail and thought about telling Ashley my secret. She knew me better than anyone, and I knew she wouldn't laugh at me. Well, she'd laugh her butt off, and then she'd try to help me. I remembered she was always interested in magical things, so I made the spot decision to tell her. If she thought I was nuts, I'd deal with that later.

I sipped the hot coffee and sighed, practically feeling the caffeine racing through my veins. I punched the return call button and waited for Ashley to pick up.

"Hey girl, how was your night? You feeling better?"

"Well, it was one heck of a night, that's all I gotta say. How about you?" I asked.

"I've had better if you know what I mean."

I snorted and continued sipping on my coffee. Well, I may as well just get it over with before I changed my mind.

"So, last night, something happened. I can talk to Razzy now."

"Your cat?"

"Yeah. I can hear her, I can understand her, and we can have a conversation now."

"Honey, I knew I should have forced you to get out more. You're too young to be a crazy cat lady."

"Ha-ha. I'm serious, Ash. I had this splitting headache, and somehow I woke up outside. Razzy found me, and I could hear her talking. Literally, I can talk with my cat."

There was silence on the other end for a split second, and then, predictably, Ashley broke into hearty guffaws that had me pulling the phone away from my ear. I patiently waited for it to pass.

"Oh girl, that's too funny. You had me going there for a second."

"Yeah, it's still true. I can talk to my cat."

Another beat of silence followed.

"Ok... You need to tell me everything that happened."

I went through my entire night with Ashley, starting with my coming home and ending with filing my story with the paper in the early hours. She listened but stayed silent. I waited, and then I couldn't take it anymore.

"So, do you think I'm insane?"

"No... I wouldn't say insane. Wow. That's a lot to take in. Did you recognize the dead guy?"

"It was pretty dark, and I didn't want to light up his face with my flashlight. No, thank you. I was more worried about getting arrested."

"You wouldn't hurt a fly. Any cop worth their salt would take one look at you and then go find a real suspect."

"Thanks. I think."

"You know what I mean. So, first things first. The talking cat thing. I don't know what to tell you, but I'm interested in what Razzy has to say. You know, you could go downtown and check out that one shop, Mystic Treasures. The owner, she's a real hippy-dippy type. She might help."

"Ash, I'm not sure I want to go admitting to the public that I can talk to my cat. I'll get locked up in the nuthouse."

"Trust me. You'll see when you meet her. Just walk in and see what happens. Now, as for the cute cop, I might have a few pointers to help you out there when you go to get your fingerprints done."

"Not interested in dating him. I just want to get cleared and get more intel for my story," I said, laughing off her offer.

"Oh, Hannah. You never change. Always work, work, and more work. Well, let me know how it goes on both counts. I've got to get dressed and kick what's his name out."

"Thanks, Ash. For everything. You're the best."

I hung up the phone and finished the last of my coffee. As I refilled my mug, Razzy strolled in, tail swaying back and forth. I felt awkward suddenly. It was one thing of being able to dream of talking to your animals. It was quite another to do it. What was I supposed to say?

"So, are you hungry?"

I figured I'd lead with food. You can't go wrong with that, right?

"I'm fine, but I need to use the litter box."

"Oh, ok. Um, don't let me stop you."

"Here's the thing, now that we can communicate, it's just a teensy bit awkward."

"You feel it too? Oh, thank God, I was thinking the same thing."

"I'm sure we'll adjust, but could I have a little privacy? Maybe later, we can talk over some new placement for the box. But for now, excuse me, I need to go."

And with that, Razzy stalked off to the corner where I kept the litter box. All righty, this was definitely interesting. I shook my head and went back to my room to get ready for the day. One quick shower later, I pulled on a pair of jeans and a long-sleeve t-shirt. I wasn't sure what was appropriate for getting your fingerprints taken, but I assumed casual would be ok.

I left my wet hair to air dry and walked back out into the living room, where Razzy was stretched out on the couch.

"Heading out?"

"Yeah, I need to go to the police station, and then I'm going to go..." I stopped, not sure if I should mention the magic store Ashley had told me about. "Run some errands. Do you need anything?"

"I'm fine. Thank you. Say hi to the cute detective for me."

"Um, sure. Well, do you want the television on or anything? Do you get bored here alone all the time?"

"Well, I usually spend my mornings meditating, and then I read on your iPad before I take my mid-morning nap."

"Wait, you meditate? And read?"

Razzy's eyes blazed, and she glared at me. Her tail started flicking back and forth.

"Yes, I read. I'm not a heathen. I also make sure I only choose free books, so you don't get charged. I'm sorry if that offends you," she said with a sniff, turning her back to me.

Who knew? Apparently, cats could read. I guess you learn something new every day.

"I'm sorry, Razzy, I didn't know. I think it's great you're well-read. You're probably smarter than I am."

"Probably?"

"You know what I mean. Well, have a good day. I'll be home as soon as I can."

I walked out of there as fast as I could and locked up behind me. This was going to take some serious getting used to. Owning a pet was one thing, but having a pet roommate who was more well-read than I was? That was a switch.

I shook my head and walked down the stairs to my car. The sun was shining brightly, and it wasn't too hot. I pushed up the sleeves on my shirt and got in my car, rolling down the windows. The police station was downtown, making it easier to find Mystic Treasures once I was done.

I really wasn't sure about opening up to a complete stranger, but I knew Ashley wouldn't steer me wrong. As I drove, I thought about what I would say to the owner. I finally settled on following the advice Ashley'd given me. Walk in, look interested in something, and see where it went from there.

Feeling like I had a plan, I pulled into the police station's parking lot and grabbed my purse. I walked in, nodding to the officer who was positioned at the front desk.

"Hi, I'm Hannah Murphy. Detective Walsh wanted me to come in and give my prints?"

"Take a seat. I'll let him know."

I sat down in one of the ratty chairs and nodded to the person sitting next to me. The magazines on the table looked like they were about eight months old, so I didn't bother grabbing one. Hopefully, I wouldn't have to wait long enough to re-read old news.

"Ms. Murphy? Follow me, please."

I looked up and saw the tall form of Ben Walsh looming over me. He was even better looking than I'd remembered. Of course, it had been pretty dark the night before. I remembered I couldn't tell what color his eyes were and made it a point to make eye contact. Ah, they were a gorgeous shade of light green.

"Where are we headed?" I asked.

"I'll have you go to the fingerprint station back here, and then I have a few more questions for you if you're not busy? I saw your story this morning, by the way. Thank you for keeping your word."

"I always do."

"That's a rarity in your profession."

Miffed he had such a low opinion of reporters, I kept my retort to myself and followed him to the back.

"Sergeant Peters here will take your prints. I'll wait."

"Miss, if you'll place your hand over the scanner, please? Keep your hand perfectly still."

"This is high tech. I was expecting the old ink pad and paper routine from when I was a kid in elementary school," I said.

The sergeant laughed.

Within a few minutes, I was freshly scanned and in the system. I looked over at Detective Walsh, and he turned to leave. I fell in behind him, unsure of what to say. Figuring silence was my best option, I walked into his office behind him.

"My cat said to say hi."

Dang it, why did I have to say that? My social anxiety reared its head at the most awkward moments, and I never knew what was going to come out of my mouth.

"Oh, that's nice. Tell her I said hi as well. Have a seat," Ben said, with a look that said he was doubting my sanity.

"Do you like cats?"

"I do. I have a cat of my own. His name is Gus. He loves to deposit his hair all over my coats."

As he said that, he picked a hair off his coat and tossed it in the can next to his desk. I thawed a little. A man who owned a cat couldn't be that bad, right?

"That's nice. I like cats."

Oh my God, Hannah, I thought to myself. Just stop.

Ben cleared his throat, and I smiled weakly, hoping he wouldn't think I was crazy.

"So, I had a few questions for you. We found several prints on the body, and I need to know where you touched the victim."

"Well, I tripped over him first, and then I poked him to see what he was. I'm not sure exactly where. Then I touched his neck to take his pulse. That's it."

"I see. I've got some photos to show you if you don't mind. We've been able to identify the victim, but we haven't notified his family yet."

"Sure, I can look."

He opened the file on his desk and laid the pictures out in front of me. As I suspected, they were of the victim. I noticed Ben watching me closely to see how I would react. I studied the pictures and glanced over at the file on the desk. Aha, he'd written the name of the victim down on the file folder tag. Filing that information away for later, I pushed the pictures back to him.

"Do you recognize him?"

"I'm sorry, I don't. Never seen him before."

He leaned back in his chair and stared at me. I was familiar with this technique. It made guilty people nervous and encouraged them to fill the quiet with chatter. Since I knew I wasn't guilty, I forced myself to keep quiet. I bit my tongue just in case my brain decided otherwise.

After a few more beats, he finally relented.

"Thanks for stopping by. I may have more questions for you at a later date."

"No problem. When will there be a press conference?"

"Press conference?"

"Yes, so the press can get more information about the crime. Who was the victim? Why was he in the park? Who had a motive for killing him?"

He grimaced at my rapid-fire questions, and stood up, motioning me towards the door.

"We'll let you know."

And I was dismissed. I walked out of his office and turned the corner, glancing back at him. He was watching me leave and immediately turned his head when he saw me catch him at it. Interesting.

I walked back out into the sunshine and pulled out my phone. I needed to find the address for Mystic Treasures. Who knew what I'd find there, but I was intrigued to see if it explained my newfound ability logically. I snorted. A logical explanation for suddenly being able to talk to cats? Ha.

The store was only a few blocks away. I pulled out from the parking lot and navigated my way through the downtown traffic. Luckily, there was a spot open right in front of the store. I parked and took a deep breath. This was going to be weird.

CHAPTER 4

*T*here was soft music playing in the store as I walked in. I noticed a heavy smell of incense that was strong, without being unpleasant. A bell chimed as the door swung shut behind me. In for a penny, in for a pound, right? I walked forward, determined to see this through.

A collection of crystals dominated the entryway, and each basket had a little card with information on it. I was leaning forward to read one when I heard a voice.

"I'll be right there."

The store seemed empty, so I assumed the voice belonged to the owner. I heard cloth swishing, and I looked up as a woman approached. Her long, wavy hair was a vibrant red, and her bright eyes were impossibly blue. She had on a simple tank top with a long patterned skirt. I noticed the strings at her waist had tiny bells that chimed as she walked.

"Hi, I'm looking for the owner. My friend, Ashley Wilson, sent me," I said, holding out my hand.

She took my hand, and her eyes shut. A look of pain flitted across her face, and she let go of my hand.

"I know Ashley. She has a kind soul. I'm Anastasia Aspen. I own the store. And you are?"

"I'm Hannah Murphy. I work for the Post with Ashley."

"I see. And how can I help you? I sense you are troubled. Many things are swirling around you. Some are good. Some are not so good."

Ok, that was typically mystical, especially from someone with the name Anastasia Aspen. That couldn't be her real name. But I wasn't really in a position to judge anyone with the whole talking to cats thing, was I?

"Well, I don't know. I experienced something that is, well, I don't know how to describe it. Ashley suggested I talk to you. You're not busy, are you? I could always come back later."

I could feel my earlier confidence fleeing the scene. Maybe this was a terrible idea. There was no way this lady was going to believe me.

"I'm always available for those who need help. It's my duty. Come, follow me to the back. I sense you need to share something that would be better if it wasn't overheard. We can share some tea."

I followed her to the back, where she had a small sofa. A tea tray with two cups was laid out on the table in front of it.

"Were you expecting someone?"

"Of course, I was. You."

Well, that was weird. It was too late to back out now, so I sank down on the sofa and put a bright smile on my face. She joined me and poured the tea into the mugs, handing me one.

"What kind of tea is this?"

"It's my blend. It's made for calming and opening up your third eye."

"Oh, I see."

I really didn't see. I looked around, taking in the many books she had on shelves. The tea was excellent, and I took another sip and tried to gather my scattered courage.

"You can tell me anything. I never judge, only advise," she said, breaking into my thoughts.

"You might judge this. I don't know where to begin."

"Begin where we all do - at the beginning."

I took a deep breath and shared my crazy experience from the day before. I was thorough, making sure I left nothing out. Everything poured out, leaving me limp once I finished my tale. I took another sip of tea.

She looked at me before picking up my hand again. I didn't miss the pain flickering there before it was gone again. She turned my hand over and examined my palm.

"Are you of Celtic descent by any chance?"

"I am, on both sides."

With my last name, it wasn't too big of a jump for her to ask me that. I waited to see what else she would say.

"Your grandmother had the sight, and your mother didn't?"

That threw me for a loop. I had never really gone into any detail on my family history with Ashley, so there was no way this lady could have known.

"That's true. How did you know?"

"It usually skips a generation. I would guess your father's grandmother also had the sight. It flows through the male side, but men rarely exhibit any gifts. It looks like you got a double scoop, so to say."

"My dad never talked much about his mother, so I'm not sure."

She gently placed my hand down on the sofa and gave it a quick pat. Her eyes closed, and she seemed as if she was in silent conversation. I wasn't sure with whom or what, but there was a vibe she was talking with someone. She nodded her head, and her blue eyes opened and focused on me.

"You've been given a rare gift. Today is the solstice, and I'm guessing you discovered this ability after midnight last night?"

"Yes, I remember looking at the time on my phone, and it was after one."

"I see. Well, my dear, the spirits have spoken, and they have chosen you. You have many tasks left to complete. It's not my place to share what those are, but what help I can give, I will share with you."

All righty, that was weird. What on earth did the spirits want with me? I was just a reporter who lived alone with my cat. I had one good friend and kept to myself.

"Did the spirits get the wrong number, so to speak? I'm not sure there's anything I can do. I'm not anything special. I'm just me."

"The spirits are wise, my dear. They never pick the wrong person. That person might let them down, but the choice is infallible."

"What am I supposed to do? I mean, it's super cool I can talk to my cat, but I don't know how that's going to change anything or make a big difference in the world or with these tasks I'm supposed to do."

"All will be revealed in time. My best guess is you are in a unique position to right wrongs, to find the truth and shed light where darkness reigns."

"I guess that clears that up, then."

Not. That was about as clear as mud. I didn't mean to come off rude, but I mean, couldn't she be a little more informative?

Anastasia laughed softly at my sarcasm. "Be patient, dear. The spirits don't follow our clocks or our ways. You'll see. In the meantime, I feel you should help solve the murder of the victim you found last night. There was a reason you discovered him."

At least that was something concrete I could do.

"Are there any other 'gifts' I can expect? Talking to my cat is awesome, but a superpower or two would be really cool. Ooo, I'd love it if I could fly."

She laughed again, shaking her head as she stood up from the sofa.

"I see many things for you, but now is not the time to reveal all. I will say this. You may be in danger. Watch yourself and use the gift that has manifested itself. Its usefulness might surprise you."

I stood to follow her back out to the main floor of the shop. I felt strangely settled as if her non-answer answers had been useful. Maybe the incense was getting to me. She stopped near the front door and turned back to face me.

"Thanks for taking the time to talk with me. I guess if you think of anything else, or if your spirits say something, let me know? I'll give you my card."

"Of course. Any time you have questions, you know where to find me. Listen to your heart and listen to your dear cat. I think she might surprise you. A whole new world has opened to you. Heed my warning and keep your heart open. Splendid things are in store."

She took my card and slipped it into the pocket of her skirt. I nodded at her and walked out, startled by the bright sunshine that made me squint. What was I supposed to do now? I walked back to my car and sat inside for a few minutes, collecting my thoughts.

Anastasia, while nice, had talked like a fortune cookie. I wasn't sure I was buying what she was selling. Pulling out onto the street, I made my way back home. I needed to do my research. Maybe I could find information on this new 'gift' and what the heck I was supposed to do with it.

My stomach growled, reminding me the waffle I'd eaten earlier this morning was long gone. Not wanting to face whatever horrific leftovers I had in my fridge, I stopped through the drive-through of a fast food place on my way home. Maybe a burger and fries would solve my problems. They couldn't hurt, right?

Within a few minutes, I was pulling into my parking lot. A quick jog up the stairs and I unlocked my door, looking around to see if Razzy was in the living room. She was curled up on the couch, deep in sleep. I put my takeout bag on the table and locked the door behind me.

"Did you get me anything?"

I jumped, still not used to hearing Razzy's soft voice.

"Um, no, I guess I didn't. Besides, I don't think you should have human food."

"A little piece of your burger would go down nicely. Just make sure there's no pepper or ketchup on it, please."

I shrugged as I grabbed a plate and walked back to the table. It was hard to argue with that logic. I tore into my meal, putting a small piece of meat aside for her. Yes, I checked it for pepper and ketchup. What can I say? I'm a pushover.

Fueled by my junk food, I cleaned up my mess and called Razzy over.

"I saved you a piece of meat, Razzy. Come on over."

"Ugh, can't you bring it over here? I'm so comfortable."

"Hey, I don't eat on the couch, and you shouldn't either."

With a long-suffering sigh, she got up, stretched, and lightly jumped down to the floor, weaving her way through my legs before sitting down at my feet. Her big blue eyes blinked up at me, and my heart melted. How could I ever stay mad at my little girl?

I gave her the meat and went into the kitchen to wash my hands. It was time to get serious about my research. First, I should look up the name I saw on the folder in Ben's office. With any luck, I'd be able to build a background on the victim and have a jump on the other reporters before the press conference on Monday.

Razzy washed her face, rubbing her paw over her whiskers before going back to the couch and getting settled on her cushion again.

I fired up my laptop and logged into our paper's portal, and pulled up our resources for running background checks. In a separate tab, I pulled up a social media search using the victim's name. Bingo! Both tabs pulled up plenty of information.

It looked like the victim, Mark Brown, had been active on social media. I pulled up his profile, thanking the god of reporters he hadn't set it to private. I grabbed a notebook from my bag and started listing out what I knew. He was active in a local softball team sponsored by a bar, he wasn't currently married, and he was definitely a player. A quick scan through his timeline showed pictures of him with several women. All of them were young, beautiful, and well-dressed.

I stopped and looked at the profile picture Mark had used. It looked like a professional headshot. I clicked on his 'about' page and saw he worked at a local bank. I opened another tab and did a search. There was a branch just a few blocks away. Given that, and the fact he'd been found dead in the park right next to my apartment, it had to mean he lived close.

I flipped back to the tab with the background check and ran through the items. I could confirm he lived in the area. A quick review of the address pulled up a swanky development of townhomes. His report was clean, no arrest records of any kind, and his credit history was spotless.

I leaned back in my chair and thought for a few minutes. He was relatively young, well off by the looks of things, athletic, and a serial dater. Why had he ended up dead? I wrote a few theories in my notebook. Was he embezzling from the bank? Was he involved in the wrong crowd? He obviously liked to party. Maybe there was a drug connection. I continued listing out my ideas and thoughts until I filled up a few pages.

I messaged Tom to let him know I had some information, but not enough to update my story yet. We couldn't run anything anyway until Mark's next of kin was notified, but I had some concrete facts I could start chasing on Monday.

I was going to close my laptop and start enjoying my weekend when I decided I should search for information on my so-called gift. Surely I couldn't be the only one who could talk to cats? Anastasia hadn't seemed too surprised by my admission. I mean, granted, she was a little out-there herself, but she hadn't batted an eye.

Typing in my search query, *ability to talk to cats*, I settled in to learn what I could. Most of the sites I pulled up were nonsensical. I found a couple of mystery books which featured talking cats, but that wouldn't do me much good. I remembered Anastasia had focused on my Celtic heritage and figured maybe that was an excellent avenue to pursue.

Before I knew it, it was getting dark. I'd lost hours perusing old folklore and mythical accounts of talking cats and the people who understood them. I wasn't sure I believed it, but it made me feel a little better. Apparently, I wasn't alone.

I closed my laptop and stood up to turn on some lights. Razzy blinked at me and yawned, exposing the back of her throat.

"Yeah, big yawn," I said, unable to avoid my ritual. Every yawn, no matter how big and every stretch, no matter how tiny, always deserved a comment.

If a cat could roll her eyes, I'd swear Razzy did. She huffed softly and changed positions on the couch.

"What are we doing tonight?"

"Well, we're not going walking in the park, I know that. I was thinking about a movie night with some delivery pizza."

"Can we watch Black Panther? I love that movie."

"Somehow, I'm not surprised. Wakanda forever!"

I used my phone to get a pizza coming and settled in for a night of watching movies with my cat. So basically a typical Saturday night for me. I softly stroked the top of Razzy's head and realized I wouldn't have it any other way.

CHAPTER 5

Monday, June 22nd

On Monday morning, I walked into the newsroom, excited to see when the press conference would be held at the police department. I tossed my bag into my cubicle and walked down the row to see if Ashley was in yet.

A glance in her cubicle told me Ashley had a long weekend. Her ordinarily flawless face featured dark bags under her eyes, and her hair was a little frizzled.

"Ashley, are you ok? You look... well, I was going to say..."

"Save it. I know I look like death warmed over. It was one hell of a weekend. I kicked what's-his-name to the curb and went down to the bar to celebrate. Before I knew it, I'd ended up with someone new, and let's just say, I think I'm gonna nickname this one the Energizer Bunny. I'm gonna keep this one! I think. Maybe not. A girl needs her beauty sleep."

"Ashley!"

"Girl, the stories I could tell you."

"No, it's fine, it's on a need-to-know basis, and I definitely don't need to know. As long as you're happy?"

"Never been happier! Now scoot, mama needs a nap before my next piece is due."

I shook my head and smiled as I walked back to my desk. As I passed by a cubicle, I heard a grating voice call out my name. Oh no, not Vinnie.

"Hey, hot stuff! What did you do all weekend?"

I rolled my eyes. Vinnie Mangione was about five feet tall and four feet wide. With the eternal optimism of a momma's boy, he thought he was God's gift to women. He just couldn't figure out why they never stuck around long enough to date. It couldn't have been because of his winning and charming personality or the fact his mother liked to oversee his dates. Huh, it's a mystery, I guess.

"Not much, Vinnie. How about you?"

"A little of this, a little of that, you know," he said, winking and wagging his eyebrows.

Is it any wonder the thought of being a cat lady appealed to me?

"Well, I hope you had fun. I gotta go," I said, trying to move past his cubicle before he could rope me into a long discussion.

"Not so fast, little lady. I saw your story over the weekend. How did you land such a prime story?"

"Well, sometimes a story falls into your lap."

Or, in my case, I literally fall over a story. Same difference, right?

"I don't buy it. You've been working fluff for so long it's coming out of your ears. Why would a nice girl like you want to be on the murder beat, anyway? You need to leave the hard work for us men and stick to writing about cooking and cleaning."

I bit my tongue and reminded myself I'd just landed a big story and the promise of more to come. I didn't need to get written up with H.R. over a fight with this guy.

"I'll keep it in mind, Vinnie. Have a good day."

I rushed past, determined to make it to my desk. Sliding into my chair, I pulled up the police department's number to see what time the presser was scheduled. A quick call with their information bureau revealed I had about an hour before it would start, giving me some time to catch up on my other assignments. I picked up the folder Tom left on my desk and started paging through the stack of papers.

It was more fluff, but knowing I had a big story in my back pocket made digesting it a little easier. I did some quick research on my laptop and outlined my stories for later.

Seeing I had just a few minutes left, I placed a call to the local bank where the victim worked and set up a time to meet with the manager right after the presser ended. From there, I planned to head to the bar that sponsored the victim's softball team.

I jotted a few notes on my laptop so I wouldn't forget and gathered up my stuff. I wanted to make it over to the police department early to snag a good spot in the press pool. Checking to make sure I had my press pass, I dashed out to my car. Today was going to be the start of something great for my career. I could just feel it.

I went over a few questions in my mind as I drove to the station. The victim's banking background might be vital, and I was feeling smug I'd gotten a jump on the other reporters. The parking lot was full, and it took me a little longer than I would've liked to find a spot. It was a little snug, but I was determined to make the best of it.

I sucked in my stomach and wedged myself out of my car, struggling not to door ding the giant pickup next to me. Mission accomplished, I snagged my bag and walked up to the front door of the station. The officer at the front desk directed me back to the press room, and I started walking faster. It was so exciting to be at my very first official press conference as a reporter!

The seats at the front were taken, so I slid into the third row, smack in the middle. This would be a good spot to take in everything. I felt someone jostle me and looked to my left. Another reporter claimed the spot next to me and sat down. He looked at me with a friendly smile.

"Hi, I'm Josh Cabot with the Trib. Never seen you here before, are you new?"

"Hi, Josh. I'm Hannah Murphy with the Post. It's my first presser.

When do you think they'll start?"

"They're usually about fifteen minutes late if we're lucky. It can drag past a half-hour most times. We're all used to it. Have you worked with the Post long?"

"About two years, after I graduated from college."

"Moving up through the ranks, then?"

"Trying to."

He nodded and opened up his laptop.

"Well, if you have questions, just ask. I'm not like the crusty old guard that wants to force new reporters to 'earn their stripes.'"

"Thanks, I'll do that."

He had a friendly, open face. His blue eyes sparkled a little as he looked back at me.

"How did you land this story?"

I didn't want to admit I'd fallen over the corpse of the victim while I was in the park in the middle of the night. This guy might be nice, but he didn't need to know all the details.

"Oh, you know, my editor assigned it to me. Guess it was my turn."

"Lucky break. Oh, hey, the new cop is running the presser. It looks like they're getting ready."

"New cop?"

"Yeah, his name is Ben Walsh. He transferred here from somewhere in California a few months ago. Just what we need, more Californians moving in. He's a by-the-booker for sure. I've been trying to figure out why he'd want to move from a plum position in a big city to this area, but I've found nothing yet. There's gotta be a reason, though."

"Hmm, interesting," I said, trying to sound noncommittal.

Ben had been all-business, but he wasn't that bad. Maybe I was being swayed by a pair of gorgeous green eyes, but I hoped for his sake that Josh wouldn't find anything terrible about Ben's past. I knew how hard it was to be a transplant, and my heart went out to him a little.

"It's starting. Nice talking with you. Maybe we can meet up for a drink sometime?" Josh asked.

"Sure, that would be nice."

I focused on the podium as Ben walked up and announced the start of the presser. He ran through the barest details of what occurred. I was thrilled he'd kept my name out of it so far. If the other reporters found out I'd been on the scene, they'd attack me like a school of piranhas.

Ben opened the floor for questions, and everyone started talking at once. One of the local television station reporters was shouting.

"Officer Walsh, can you go into more detail about how the body was discovered?"

Ben's eyes briefly met mine. I bit my lip, praying he'd keep quiet.

"As of right now, we're holding back the name of the person who discovered the body. They wish to remain anonymous."

"Why are you protecting them? Were they involved in the crime? Did they know the victim?"

That was from another television reporter. I scanned around the room, trying to place which one had asked the question.

"We have no further information to release," Ben said.

I let out a sigh and noticed Josh was staring at me. I smiled and hoped he'd brush off my reaction as being new to the game. Josh raised his hand and spoke up.

"Can you release the name of the victim?"

"Yes, the victim was a local man by the name of Mark Brown. Are there more questions?"

"Officer Walsh, do you have any leads or a motive for why someone would want this man dead?"

"I'm unable to share that information. Thank you for coming."

Ben walked off the stage, and the press corps started shouting over each other. The sound was deafening, and I moved to stand. It was disappointing nothing new had come up at the conference, but I'd spent the weekend getting my story prepped with what I already knew. A quick polish of it, and I'd have it ready to go for tomorrow's edition.

As I moved down the aisle, I felt a hand on my arm. I looked back and saw Josh smiling at me.

"About that drink?"

"Oh, sorry, I'm tied up today. Maybe some other time?"

His face fell and I felt terrible, but I needed to get this story posted and finish my assignments.

"Ok, well, I'm sure I'll see you around," Josh said, turning to leave.

He seemed like such a nice guy. He wasn't my type, but it was always good to have friends. I stopped him before he could get out of the aisle.

"Hey, can I have your number? I'll call sometime," I said.

He shot me a grin and took a small pad of paper out of his shirt pocket. He scribbled his number on it and stuck it in my bag.

"Talk to you soon, Hannah."

I slid past the chairs of the aisle and moved out into the hallway. Ben was standing in a cluster of cops, and I nodded as I moved past. I felt a hand on my arm and stopped. Geez, what was it with people grabbing my arm today?

"Ms. Murphy, wait."

I looked up into Ben's impossibly green eyes and felt my stomach flutter a little. Why did he have to be so handsome?

"Yes?"

He ran his hand through his hair, leaving the top ruffled.

"I just wanted to thank you for not publishing anything else on the case and waiting for the press conference. It means a lot you kept your word."

"I always do. And thanks for not throwing me to the wolves in there. If they'd found out I'd discovered the body, I'm not sure what would've happened."

"I debated on it. But you seem honest. As long as you keep your word, I'll do my best to protect you. You're not from here, are you?"

"No, I'm from South Dakota. I came here for college and never left."

We looked at each other awkwardly for a second as more reporters streamed past us. I didn't know what to think of his extra attention.

"Well, I'll let you go. Thanks again," Ben said, turning back to the other cops.

"No problem."

I walked outside, mentally reviewing my story, completely lost in thought. A voice shouting at me startled me out of my daze.

"Hey, you! Who are you?"

I turned to see who was shouting at me. It was an older man, with a rumpled shirt and a stained tie. His balding head shone in the sunlight. It took me a second to recognize him from the picture that accompanied his byline. The photo must have been about twenty years old. It was Dave Freidrich, a reporter for the biggest paper in town, our chief competitor.

"I'm Hannah Murphy. I work for the Post."

"Hmph. I see. Well, I'd like to know how you got the jump on us and got your story in so fast. I monitor the scanner, and by the time I got to the park they were wrapping up their investigation. How did your story get in so fast? It was on the website within minutes and in print the next morning."

"Well, let's just say technology is a reporter's best friend," I said, moving to walk past him.

"I'm watching you. You won't get the jump on me again. This is my turf," he said with a sneer. "This is real man's work. It's not for little girls like you. Go home and focus on what you know best."

I won't lie. I was a little shaken at how vehement he was. Tiny flecks of spittle flew while he was talking. Gross, right? Still, I wouldn't let this guy bully me.

"Tell you what, Mr. Freidrich. You write your story, and I'll write mine. We'll see who gets the better scoop."

I walked past him quickly and squeezed between the truck to get to my door.

"Don't you scratch my truck!"

I should have known he was the owner of the monster parked next to me. A tiny part of me wanted to bash my door against the side of it, but my better side won. I sidled into my car and threw it in reverse. What? If he didn't want to get run over, he should probably get out of my way.

I checked the time on my dash and saw I had a few minutes left to get to the bank for my appointment with the manager. I merged onto the street and prayed traffic would be light.

CHAPTER 6

*H*ave I ever mentioned how much I hate waiting? Well, I have now. I made it to the bank with minutes to spare, and for the past forty-five minutes, I've been sitting here, cooling my jets. Why do banks always have the most uncomfortable chairs in their waiting rooms? I'd already blown through the brochures they had stacked around, and even though I was bored to tears, I now knew the importance of savings. Yay!

As I was about to give up and try to reschedule, a man wearing a suit that cost more than I made in a month walked up. His bland face creased into an approximation of a smile.

"Miss Murphy?"

"Yes?"

"Sorry about the wait. I'm Gerald Harms, the manager of the branch. You had an appointment with me? Please, follow me."

Finally! I grabbed my bag and followed Harms down the hall, glancing in the offices as I walked. We passed a closed door, and I noticed the nameplate read Mark Brown, so I slowed my pace to peek inside. Everything was tidy. The only thing on his desk was a bright blue binder with tabs. I wished I could get my hands on it.

At the end of the hall, Harms held out his arm and directed me into his office. I sank into the cushy chair across from his desk. Aha, this is where they've been keeping the comfortable chairs.

"So, Miss Murphy, how can I help you today? My secretary said you had some questions?"

"Yes, I'm a reporter with the Post. I'm doing a story on Mark Brown, and I wanted to know more about his background and work here. It's a human-interest piece that'll focus on who he was as a person before he was murdered."

I watched for his reaction to the name. A slight look of distaste flickered across his face before it returned to its usual bland state. Interesting.

"I see. Well, I'm not sure what I can tell you. Mark worked here for five years and moved up through the ranks quickly. He was a loan officer with us in our commercial division."

"What can you tell me about him?"

There had to be more than just the standard line of being a good worker, blah, blah, and blah. He worked with Mark for five years. Hopefully, I could get him to open up a little more.

"I'm not sure what you're asking."

"Did you enjoy working with him? Was he a fun guy to be around?"

Harms shifted in his chair, playing with his tie. His gaze dropped, and he didn't look me in the eye as he answered.

"You could say he was the office jokester. He was always laughing, never too serious. His clients loved him."

So, his clients loved him, but maybe not his co-workers. I kept reading between the lines, trying to figure out what Harms wasn't saying. I could tell from his body language he was uncomfortable.

"Was he difficult to work with? Was he ever in any trouble?" I asked.

His eyes narrowed, and the look of distaste was back. This time, it hung around.

"Define trouble. Did he go through the tellers like they were candy? Definitely. Did he enjoy flirting with the wives of our senior staff at company get-togethers? Every time. But as for his accounts, his clients were happy, and he brought a lot of business into our bank."

Ok, now we were getting somewhere. I wondered if his wife had been a recipient of Mark's flirtation. It sounded like the bank put up with Mark's antics thanks to the money flowing through his accounts.

"Was there ever any sign of any illicit activities in any of his accounts?"

Harms flushed bright red and squeezed his hands before catching himself and spreading them out on the table. Bingo! I'd hit a nerve.

"I'm afraid I can't answer that question. Now, if that's all, I have another appointment," he said, gritting his teeth.

I knew better than to push too hard. I needed to find someone with an inside connection to this bank who could get more details. It was clear something was going on, but I couldn't get anywhere with this guy.

"Thanks for your time, Mr. Harms. I appreciate it."

I left his office and walked back to my car. Where was I going to find someone who was privy to the information I needed? My best guess would be at the bar where Mark hung out. He'd posted dozens of pictures on his social media accounts from the bar. With any luck, it was a company hang-out. Sitting in my car, I turned on the engine and rolled down the windows as I searched for the address for Dingers, the name of the bar. Luckily, they opened in just a few minutes.

By the time I reached the bar, I realized I was starving. I pulled into their parking lot and saw a few cars parked there. The smell of burgers cooking on a grill confirmed they served food. My stomach gave an appreciative rumble as I walked inside.

It took a few seconds for my eyes to adjust to the gloom inside. A few tables were scattered around, but all the patrons were at the bar. I took my cue from them and grabbed a stool. The bartender waved over at me, acknowledging my presence as I sat down. There was a menu card on the bar top, and I slid it over, seeing what they had on special. Monday's special was a patty melt with curly fries. That sounded good to me.

"What can I get you?"

I looked up at the bartender, pegging her age at about mid-40s. Her blonde hair was tied back in a high ponytail, and her eye makeup was a work of art. Oh, for the ability to do a cat's eye like she could. Her name tag read Jolie.

"I'll take the special and a Coke, please."

"Sure thing. I haven't seen you in before."

"It's my first time. Nice place."

She shrugged and looked noncommittal. "Anything else I can get you?"

"That's it for now, thanks."

She walked back towards the kitchen window and shouted my order through it before bringing back my drink.

I watched her wipe down the bar, and I sipped on my Coke. Since no one was demanding her attention, I figured now was a great time to see if she knew anything about Mark.

"Have you worked here long?" I asked.

"I've been here for seven years. Why?"

"Oh, I was just wondering if you knew someone who came in here a lot. Mark Brown's his name."

She snorted and tossed the towel over her shoulder.

"He knock you up, honey?"

"What? No, I'm a reporter with the Post. I'm doing a story on him."

"Did he finally poke the wrong guy's wife and end up dead?"

"That may not be far from the truth. He was found dead in a park not from here over the weekend."

Her face went through a myriad of emotions as she digested what I'd just said.

"Wait, he's dead?"

"Yes, I'm sorry I'm the one to tell you. Were you close?"

Another snort and the towel came back down as she mechanically wiped the bar top.

"No, we weren't close. I'm just surprised he's gone. He wasn't a terrible guy. He could be funny. I've seen him every happy hour for the past two years. It just seems crazy he won't be coming in. Wow."

A shout came from the kitchen. I couldn't make out what was said, but apparently, Jolie understood. She walked back, grabbed the plate, and delivered it to a guy at the end of the bar. After a few seconds, she walked back over to me.

"So, do you know what happened? Was anyone arrested?" she asked.

"No arrests yet. He was found on Saturday morning."

"Huh. He'd been here Friday night. My shift ends at eight, and he was still here when I left. He'd been getting cozy with a new chick."

"What did she look like?"

"This one had red hair. I couldn't tell you for sure what eye color she had. Maybe brown? She was pretty. His girls always were."

"Had you seen her before?"

"Yeah, she always comes in with the bank crew. This is their hang-out. If you come back after five, you'll probably run into a few of them. Most nights, at least a handful come in."

Another shout issued from the kitchen and Jolie walked back to grab my food. She slid it in front of me.

"Thanks, this looks good."

"Want any ketchup?"

"Sure."

I dug into my patty melt, savoring the melty cheese clinging to the crispy rye bread. It was better than I'd expected. By the time I was mopping up the remaining ketchup with my last fry, Jolie had returned.

"Anything else?"

"No, that was awesome, though. I'll come back for sure."

I grabbed my wallet and slid two twenties across the bar.

"Need any change?"

"No, that's for you."

"Thanks, that's nice of you," she said, as she tucked the bills in her apron pocket and looked at me with her head tilted. "You know, I remembered the name of the girl Mark was with before he left. I don't know if it will help, but her name is Rita Matthews. I think she's a teller at the bank."

"That's helpful. If you know a few of the other people he hung out with, I'd appreciate it."

"Sure, honey, don't see how it will hurt. He wasn't the world's best guy, but no one deserves to die alone like that. If it helps you find who killed him, I'm happy to help. Let me go take care of that guy down there, and I'll be right back."

I took my notebook and a pen out of my bag as I waited. This lunch visit had been way more profitable than my interview with the bank manager. Jolie walked back over and listed out a few names for me. I wrote everything down and slid my notebook back into my bag. There were enough names there to keep me busy for a while. I thanked her and walked back out into the bright sunshine.

My eyes hadn't yet adjusted, and I bumped into someone entering the bar. Whoever I hit was built like a Mack truck. I shaded my eyes and looked up into the green eyes of Ben Walsh. Oh great, just who I wanted to run into.

"I see you've been doing your homework, Ms. Murphy. Fancy seeing you here."

"Um, they have a great patty melt," I said, with a weak smile.

"Right. Just like you must have an account with the First Legacy bank a few blocks away."

"Are you following me?"

"I was pulling in the parking lot there and saw you leaving. Pretty strange coincidence you were at the spot where the victim worked."

"What can I say? I'm good at research."

He looked at me closely, and I took an involuntary step back as I realized how close I was standing to him. Close enough to get a whiff of the sandalwood scent clinging to his clothes. What? This guy smelled way too good. I couldn't help it.

"Interesting how you've got the jump on everyone else. Almost like you had advance information."

"Yeah, crazy world we're living in," I said as I backed away. "Amazing what you can find on the Internet. Well, see you around, Detective!"

I hurried back to my car, glancing back as I turned the corner into the parking lot. Ben was still standing there, watching me. Thankfully, by the time I pulled out onto the street, he was gone. I let out a breath I hadn't realized I was holding.

Where now? I needed to run backgrounds on the list of names I had. I could go back to the office or run home and check on Razzy. Time with my cat definitely beat time spent avoiding Vinnie Mangione, so I steered my car towards home.

Razzy gave a little chirp as I opened the door, and she rushed over to me. That little sound made me inexplicably joyful. I relished being able to have a conversation with her, but I would've missed the little sounds she made. Apparently, there wasn't an English equivalent of her chirp, which made me glad. It wouldn't have been the same.

I stroked her back as she wove around my legs as I slowly made my way over to the table.

"Mama, where have you been? I missed you," Razzy said, purring at the same time. She sniffed the air. "Did you have a patty melt for lunch? Did you bring me back any?"

Uh oh, I didn't consider her powerful nose. For a second, I felt terrible I'd forgotten to save her some, but then again, she didn't need human food, right?

"I did, Razzy. I'm sorry I didn't bring you any."

Her eyes rounded, and if she could've cried, I think she would have. She turned her back to me and stalked towards the couch.

"I see how it is. I sit here, alone, all day, with nothing to do. Starving. And you feast while you're gone, forgetting your poor little cat. Your poor, hungry little cat."

I rolled my eyes. I'd always thought she tended towards being a drama queen, and this little speech confirmed it.

"Why didn't you read a book if you were bored? You said you like to read. And don't pull the starving cat routine with me. You've got plenty of cat food in your bowl. You know you shouldn't eat too much human food. It's not good for you."

She whipped her head around at me, glaring for a beat before softening.

"Touché," she said as she hopped on the couch, turning around to get comfortable. "What else did you do today?"

I sat next to her, stroking her head as I told her about my day so far. Her ears perked in interest as I described my meeting with the bank manager and what Jolie had said.

"So, it sounds like he was quite the playboy. My money's on the bank manager. I bet Mark was playing back alley bingo with his wife, and he killed him for it."

I couldn't help but laugh. Not only was my cat well versed in the inner workings of human affairs, but her terminology was hilarious.

"Back alley bingo? Where did you pick that up?"

"I read a lot. By the way, can you get that subscription book thingy? There are only so many free books out there. I think they let you read unlimited books for one monthly fee."

"I'll see what I can do."

"Thanks, I'd appreciate it. Now, it's time for my mid-afternoon nap. If you're going to do your research here, could you do it quietly? It always sounds like you're using a machine gun when you type."

I chuckled as I gave her a final pat on the head before heading over to the table to get my laptop. As I opened it and started typing, Razzy cracked an eye open at me. I obediently softened my fingers and tried to type quietly. This is what my life has come to, I guess. And you know what? That's ok with me.

I spent the next few hours pulling backgrounds on the list of names Jolie had supplied. It looked like it was a cast of colorful characters, and at first glance, a few might have motives to kill Mark.

Of the six people I had on my list, half of them worked at the bank. Rita Matthews was a teller there, which meant I couldn't interview her at work. I made a note to track her down at the bar. Georgia North and Wesley Laughlin both worked as lenders, so I assumed I'd be able to set up appointments with them.

That left the three remaining people on my list. Tim Waters, who featured heavily in Mark's social timelines, was a member of the gym Mark used to attend. I could probably find him there. Lanie Edwards used to be a teller at the bank. Maybe I could track her down at the bar as well. Jordan Peters, his ex-girlfriend, was a little harder to pin down. It appeared she was an Instagram influencer. Did influencers have offices? Where did they do their influencing?

Feeling like I had a good plan, I updated my story, featuring some background on the victim. With a unique spin, I hoped I could make this story something special. Take it beyond the standard so-and-so was murdered type of story and bring out the human element.

I shrugged my shoulders and hit send in our company portal. I'd find out soon enough if Tom agreed with my take on it. That left finishing up the fluff assignments I'd been given. I browsed through my notes, grimacing until one caught my interest. It featured a new jewelry store opening in town, and the name was familiar.

A glance at the Instagram profile of Jordan Peters confirmed I had just seen it. She was scheduled to be at the opening tomorrow as a celebrity guest. Score! I put a reminder on my phone so I'd be there early. With any luck, I could take Jordan aside and interview her.

"Are you going to work all night?"

My head snapped up as I heard Razzy's soft voice at the foot of my chair. I hadn't heard her jump down from the couch.

"Geez, you scared me! No, I just need to set up some interviews for tomorrow, and then I'll be done for the day. Why?"

"Just curious. And hungry. What's for supper?"

"I'll make a few calls, and then we'll pick out a can of food for you. Is that ok?"

Razzy licked the fur of her ruff and considered my offer. She sighed and sank next to my feet.

"I guess so. I have little choice. It's not like I have thumbs and can open my can of food. I must wait on your whims. It's been so long since I ate."

I couldn't help but laugh. Before I could understand her, she'd made her feelings known on her food schedule with piteous little mews. Now, I had the full benefit of her particular brand of sarcasm. I shook my head and ruffled the fur on her head.

"Five minutes, I think you'll make it that long."

I dialed up the bank and asked to speak to Georgia first. She intrigued me. There wasn't much on her background, and I wanted to see why she was on Jolie's list. I got through to her right away and set up a time to meet her at lunch. She picked a small café near the bank. I moved on to Wesley and booked a time with him at the bank in the afternoon. Tomorrow was going to be a busy day.

CHAPTER 7

Tuesday, June 23rd

*W*hy is it when you make plans the night before, your bed seems to become a million times more inviting the next morning? By the time it registered in my sleep-fogged brain that I needed to get to the jewelry store to interview Jordan Peters and cover the opening for my assignment, I only had fifteen minutes left to get ready.

Razzy sat on the edge of the bed, amusement clear in the quirk of her whiskers as she watched me hustle back and forth, talking to myself.

"Why did you hit snooze so many times?"

"I can't help it, Razzy. You were so warm, and we stayed up half the night talking. I didn't want to move."

"Humans. You take so long to get moving. Us cats, we can go from sound asleep to wide awake in the blink of an eye."

"Don't rub it in! As it is, I'll be lucky to get any coffee in me before

I have to meet Jordan. Well, wish me luck," I said as I gathered my things up and prepared to head out the door.

"I wish I could go with you and help solve this case. It gets old being locked up here, day after day," Razzy said, her eyes rounded and pleading.

I stopped in my tracks. She knew exactly which card to pull to make me feel guilty. I'd discussed the case with her the night before, and she'd had some interesting insights. Who knew cats were so tuned in to how humans operated?

"I'll figure something out, I promise! I've gotta go, traffic will probably be crazy and I'll end up being late."

I rushed out the door with a final wave and jogged down the steps to the parking lot. There had to be some sort of bag I could get that would double as a cat carrier and not be too obvious. Now that I understood just how bright Razzy was, it seemed cruel to leave her home all alone. I shook off my thoughts and opened the door of my Blazer, sliding in and throwing it in reverse.

Thanks to some back road shortcuts, I made it to the jewelry store with about two minutes to spare. I noticed they had some signs up in their parking lot proclaiming their grand opening, but so far, it looked pretty sparse. Grabbing my bag, I slid out and walked up, wishing I'd had a little more time to make myself presentable. Well, only one person to blame for that, I guess.

The jewelry store's interior was quiet, and I saw three women with name tags clustered around the cash register. As the bell above the door dinged to announce my entry, they turned as one, eyes lighting up. Now I knew what a mouse felt like when cats surround it.

"Welcome to the Jewelry Box," one girl said as they jostled to get around the counter.

"Um, hi, I'm with the Post. I'm doing a story on your grand opening."

All three faces fell, and their eager expressions were replaced with dull boredom. Once again, they turned as one back to their discussion. Were they some sort of non-identical triplets? If I'm being honest, it was a little creepy. But then again, I watch a lot of bad horror movies.

"Oh, you'll want to talk to the owner. She's in the back with Jordan getting prepped," the second girl said, dismissing me with a wave towards a hallway behind the desk.

I went down the hall and turned left into an office. Seated at the desk was a beautiful woman who I'd pegged to be around 60. Sitting across from her was Jordan Peters, who was even prettier in person. One look at her flawless makeup, hair, and outfit made me feel instantly underdressed and out of place. I hurriedly squashed down those feelings and put on a bright smile.

"Hi, I'm Hannah Murphy, with the Post. I'm here to cover your grand opening."

An inelegant sound came from Jordan's chair, but I wasn't sure I could believe such a flawless creature could make that kind of noise. I noticed the bag under her seat was moving alarmingly. A small, furry head popped out and made the same sound again. She had a pug in her purse!

"Jordan, I told you not to bring that filthy creature with you today. Sorry, dear. Hannah, was it? I'm Kim Thatcher. I own this store. Thanks so much for coming by."

"Not a problem. Do you have a few minutes to talk about your plans?" I asked.

"Of course, of course. Jordan, why don't you go up front and prepare for the crowds? I think we have a good game plan put together."

Jordan stood in a graceful motion and slung her bag over her shoulder. The poor pug inside looked like it had some pretty severe motion sickness, and I worried it was going to yak all over me. I tried to smile as Jordan moved past, wafting an overpowering smell of perfume that made my nose twitch.

"Sounds good, Kimmy. I'll see you soon. Say bye, Pookie-kins," Jordan said, holding the dog's paw up in a wave. She exited the room as her dog made a weird sound again.

"If I've told that girl once, I've told her a thousand times to leave that smelly pug at home. I swear. The things I do for the kids of my friends. Now, dear, you said you have some questions?"

"Do you know Jordan's mom?"

"Yes, I've known Jordan since she was a chubby thirteen-year-old with crooked teeth and pimples everywhere."

I raised an eyebrow.

"Surely, someone like Jordan never went through an awkward stage. She's so perfect."

"All that glitters isn't gold, that's all I have to say. Sometimes it's just cheap tin with a good coat of paint. Now, let me give you some background on my store," Kim said, settling back in her chair.

I shrugged off my envy and remembered I was here to do a story. I took notes as Kim filled me in on her dream of owning a jewelry store and everything she'd put in to make it a success. As I listened, I felt terrible that so far, the turnout hadn't been great. She seemed like a genuinely lovely person. With any luck, it would pick up later in the day.

Once I had what I needed to write my piece, I thanked Kim and went back out onto the store's main floor. I spotted Jordan leaning against a display case, fixing her makeup. Between the overly long eyelashes, her alarmingly large chest, and sky-high heels, she was a modern marvel of balance. Her bag was next to her, and the pug was snoring loudly. Briefly, I wondered if my new ability with cats also meant I could talk to dogs.

"Jordan? Do you have a minute?" I asked.

She made a popping sound with her lips as she finished applying a fresh coat of lipstick.

"Sure, why not? It's not like this place has anything going on," she said with a shrug.

"I wanted to ask about your relationship with Mark Brown. I don't know if you heard..."

"Yeah, I heard he's dead. It didn't surprise me, really. He couldn't stay faithful if someone locked him in a chastity belt. You get what's coming to you, I always say."

She flicked her long hair over her shoulder and looked bored. A loud doggy emission punctuated the snoring of her pug in the background. I tried hard to keep it together.

"What can you tell me about Mark? All I'm hearing is he got around, but not much about who he was as a person. You dated him for a long time, right?"

"I guess. I mean, he was fun to be around. He knew people who knew people, so I put up with it for as long as possible. I've put a lot of work into building up my following, and it never hurts to meet the right people. He was hot, and it was good for my image. After a few months, he got kinda weird. I cut him loose after that."

"What do you mean he got weird?"

She studied her nails before answering me. I noticed they were shaped like stilettos with alarmingly sharp points. How on earth could this girl function with nails like that? I'd poke my eye out in fifteen minutes flat.

"I dunno, he got really jumpy and paranoid. He was always asking if I was looking at his phone. He worked late a lot and just kinda checked out of our relationship. I'm going places, you know, I don't need to be dragged down by a weirdo."

"Do you think it was something he was involved with at work?"

"Could be. I never really paid attention, I guess. Is that all? I need to go powder my nose. Would you mind watching Pookie-kins for a second?"

And with that, she was gone in another cloud of perfume. I shook my head and glanced down. The pug was awake and panting loudly.

"Hey, Pookie-kins, what's up?" I asked, figuring now was as good a time as any to see if I could understand dogs.

Nothing. He looked at me vacantly and swiped an overly long tongue around his muzzle. So just cats then, I guess. I looked around the store, pleased to see a few more people streaming in. Kim might have a good opening after all.

"Thanks, doll," Jordan said as she reappeared next to me.

Her eyes were dilated, and she swiped at her nose quickly. I didn't miss the telltale white dust around her nostrils before she rubbed it away. Interesting.

"Well, thanks for your time," I said.

She nodded in my direction before straightening her shoulders and flashing a megawatt grin at the people standing around. I guess it must have been show-time.

As I walked back out to my car, I laughed at my initial reaction to Jordan. Even though she appeared perfect, I still wouldn't trade who I was, even if I was short and scrawny. Sometimes, perfection isn't all it's cracked up to be.

A glance at my watch confirmed I had just enough time to make it to the café Georgia North had picked for our meeting. My stomach rumbled, reminding me I'd once again skipped breakfast.

I made it to the café early and let the hostess know I was meeting someone. She showed me to a booth, and I slid in to wait. I pulled out my laptop and started putting my piece together for the jewelry store while it was still fresh in my head. Completely engrossed in my work, I startled when I heard Georgia's voice above me.

"Hannah Murphy? I thought I recognized you from your picture in the paper. I'm Georgia North."

"Hi, Georgia, please sit down. I'm just working on another story," I said as I slid my laptop back into my bag.

Georgia looked like the prototypical professional. A dark pantsuit, crisply pressed, check. A silk blouse with a bow at the neck, double-check. Fashionably highlighted hair that probably wouldn't move if an F-5 tornado rumbled through the cafe, triple check. Everything about her screamed, 'I work in a bank, and you can trust me.' Hopefully, I could.

She sat across from me, placing her bag in the booth's corner.

"Have you ordered already?" she asked.

"No, I was waiting for you. I think our server is coming over now."

We put in our orders for lunch, and I waited until we were alone to ask questions. I was planning where to start when she broke into my thoughts.

"So, I'm guessing you want to discuss Mark Brown?"

"Actually, yes, I do. I was given your name as someone who knew him. I've been working on a story about his life."

"I know, Gerald Harms was talking about your interview the other day. He didn't want any of us to talk to you about bank business, but who's he to tell me what to do? If you want to know something, I'm here to help."

Well, this was interesting. Apparently, she had an ax to grind. I could use this to get a clearer picture of the motives behind Mark's death. The only thing I wondered was if she was too ready to throw some stones. What about her own glass house? This was going to be interesting.

"What can you tell me about working with Mark?"

"On the surface, he was a good employee. He brought in a ton of clients and always seemed to close new deals. He moved through the ranks quickly. At first, I thought he was just good at his job, but the past few months really had me thinking."

"Thinking about what?"

"The clientele he was bringing in changed. At first, it was local business people, but then it changed to people who weren't from the community. Why did people from California need to borrow money from our bank here in Colorado when they don't have any interests here? I brought my concerns to Harms, but he brushed me off. Honestly, now that Mark is gone, the bank is going to take a big hit to our revenue numbers."

"Did you ever suspect he might be involved in anything shady?"

Georgia carefully put her hands on the table, palms down, and took a deep breath. She tucked her hair behind her ear and looked out the window. It took her a few seconds to answer.

"I suppose I should mention that three months ago, I got passed up for a promotion. It went to Mark. I'll admit it wasn't my finest moment. I was determined to get even, so I did a little digging into his book of business."

Aha! Maybe we were finally getting somewhere. I leaned forward, eager for her to finish.

"Did you find anything?"

"I found a few discrepancies, but then I felt so bad about what I was doing I quit looking. Maybe I was just bitter, you know? He was such a young kid, and to see him be so successful rankled. I felt like a mean old hag, and I didn't like it. I've worked for this bank for a long time, but I just transferred here from another branch a year ago. I'm not really part of their club, so to speak. I figured I'd focus on my job instead of worrying about what Mark was doing."

"Did that work out for you?"

She looked away again, and a flush started creeping up from the tie on her silk blouse. Her lips thinned into a line, and her eyes hardened.

"I got passed up again last week. It is tough being a woman in this business. No one takes you seriously."

"Would you be willing to do a little more digging into what Mark was doing? You don't have to say yes, but it might help track down who killed him."

I was hoping like crazy she'd say yes. I needed someone inside the bank who could access their files. Between what Jordan had said and this new information, it sure sounded like the last few months of Mark's life had taken an interesting turn.

We were interrupted by the server delivering our food. I blinked as I took in the size of my club sandwich. It was bigger than my head and the plate could hardly contain it, let alone the pile of french fries. Georgia had ordered the Cobb salad and was picking at it as I tried to maneuver half of my sandwich into my mouth.

Silence reigned for a few minutes, but I could tell she was considering my question. I let her stew, hoping she'd want to fill the silence. Dipping a fry in ketchup, I watched her out of the corner of my eye.

"I'll do it. It might take a few days, but I'll see if I can find anything for you. You've got to keep my name out of it, though."

I nodded as I wiped the mayo off my mouth. Clubs were awesome, but dang, they were difficult to eat.

"I'll keep your name completely out of it. I appreciate your help. This could help solve Mark's murder."

She shrugged and continued picking at her lunch. I finished half the club and saved the rest of my meal for later. The server came back, and I asked for the bill and a container for my food. I noticed Georgia had barely touched hers.

"Did you want a container too? I should have asked our server."

"No, I'm not that hungry," she said, as she pushed her plate to the edge of the table.

I grabbed a card from my bag and passed it over to her.

"If you find something, or if you remember anything you think might be helpful, just call me."

"Will do. I've got to get going. I've got a meeting at the bank. Maybe now that Mark's gone, I'll get a shot at some bigger clients."

I nodded and watched as she slid out of the booth. Her heels tapped on the tile floor as she left. I pulled out my notebook and wrote a few thoughts on our meeting. On the surface, she didn't strike me as someone who would kill to get ahead, but she stood to gain a lot with Mark's death.

I had plenty of time before my next meeting with Wesley Laughlin at the bank. I grabbed my things and headed out to my car, figuring I'd stop at a local pet shop and see if I could find a carrier for Razzy.

CHAPTER 8

*T*he selection of pet carriers made me giggle as I tried to picture myself carrying Razzy around. My favorite had to be the backpack with a large, transparent bubble for a cat to look out. Even though I was tempted, if just to see Razzy's reaction to it, I put it back. I finally settled on a backpack with a compartment I could use for my notebook and laptop and a nice cozy spot for Razzy with a screened opening. If you didn't look too closely, you'd never know there was a cat in there.

I paid for my new carrier and headed over to the bank for my meeting with Wesley. So far, the cast of characters in Mark Brown's life had been fascinating, and I couldn't help but wonder what Wesley would be like in person. I pulled into the parking lot and breezed through the bank, hoping Gerald Harms wasn't around to spot me.

Wesley's office was next to the one that had belonged to Mark. I peeked inside, noticing it'd been cleared out. I knocked on Wesley's door before walking in. He was on the phone and held up a finger to tell me to wait. I took a seat and watched him as he talked.

He looked about the same age as Mark Brown, and something told me the streaks running through his blonde hair weren't natural. He was tanned, and his white teeth gleamed out of his face. His tie was loosened around his neck, and he had his sleeves rolled up, revealing a set of toned forearms. I tried to listen to his conversation without appearing too interested.

From the banking jargon he was tossing around, I'd guessed he was talking to a potential client. I'll admit, after the third API, I tuned out. Luckily, he wrapped up his call and turned his attention to me before I fell asleep in the chair.

"Hi, I'm Wesley Laughlin," he said, sticking his hand across his desk. "You're with the Post, right? Hannah Murphy?"

"That's me. Thanks for agreeing to meet with me. I hope you have time for just a few questions."

"Ask away. Anything I can do to help my old buddy, I'm happy to do it."

Interesting. He didn't mention the moratorium Gerald Harms had put out on me. I wondered if Georgia had been telling the truth.

"What can you tell me about Mark as a person? I gather you were friends with him?"

Wesley leaned back and stretched, putting his arms behind his head. Judging from how the fabric pulled taut across his arms, he was a frequent gym user. He flashed another blinding smile at me.

"We were good friends. We played on the same softball team and went to the same gym. I knew him pretty well, I think."

"I see. Did you notice anything different about him before he passed away?"

"No, not really. He was the same old fun guy. We partied the weekend before and had a blast. I had to work late on Friday, or I would have been at the bar with him," he said, suddenly frowning. "Guess if I'd gone, that could have been me."

"Any reason you think you would have been targeted?" I asked.

He startled out of his reverie and put his smile back on.

"No, just saying, you know. One of those crazy things."

"Do you know anyone who would have wanted him dead?"

"No, everyone loved the guy. He was a class act. I always wished I could be as good of a lender as he was. He got all the great deals."

"Did you ever notice anything off here at the bank? Any deals that might have been a little too good to be true?"

"Not at all. He was above-board all the way."

I could see I wouldn't get very far with this guy. Every answer was a non-answer, painted up to look pretty, but with no real substance underneath. As I stood up to leave, I noticed two things on his desk. First, he had a picture of Jordan on his desk. Second, I noticed the blue binder I'd last seen on Mark's desk was now sitting on his.

I sat back down and went for the throat.

"So, it looks like you're moving in on a few things that used to be Mark's, huh? His ex-girlfriend and his book of business?"

His smile slipped back off his face, and his eyes glinted in a way I didn't like. The good-natured frat-boy act was replaced by something more sinister. Nailed it! My guess that the binder contained Mark's old clients paid off.

"I'm sure I don't know what you mean," he said, cracking his neck.

"I think you do. I think you stand to profit quite a lot from Mark's death. It's always a little awkward to date a buddy's ex while he's still around, isn't it? It's also hard to get ahead when your buddy's getting all the best clients."

"I think it's time for you to leave, Ms. Murphy."

"I think it's time for you to tell the truth."

His eyes narrowed, and for a hot second, I thought he was going to come across the desk. Suddenly, his demeanor changed, and the smile was back. He visibly relaxed and leaned back in his chair.

"That's what I've been doing, Hannah. If I'm dating Jordan, it's not a big deal. He was done with her a long time ago, and he didn't mind at all. You've got it all wrong. In fact, I know my buddy would've wanted me to take care of his clients if something happened to him."

If I hadn't just witnessed his drastic personality change, I might have believed him. As it was, I decided now was the perfect time to leave. I definitely had more information than I started with and a new suspect to add to my list. With any luck, I could get Georgia to look at the binder and see if she found anything interesting. I stood up and walked towards the door.

"Thanks for your time, Mr. Laughlin. If I have any more questions, I will get in touch with you."

"You do that."

As I walked out into the bank's lobby, I noticed the tellers were closing up their windows for the day - what a perfect time to head to their local bar. I could work on my story while I waited for the bank crew to show up.

Within a few minutes, I was set up at a table near the bar, working on my laptop. Hopefully, the bank tellers would be true to form and would arrive shortly, ready to blow off some steam from their day. In the meantime, I had a story to file. I didn't see Jolie, which was a bummer. The bartender on duty was taciturn and didn't seem to want to answer questions when I'd first arrived.

I entered my story into the portal and texted Ashley to see how her day was going. I'd been so wrapped up in chasing down leads for this story, I hadn't been at the office much, and I missed her. She texted me right back with a hilarious story about another reporter on staff. As I waited, I noticed a girl sitting alone at another table. She was eyeing the door almost as much as I was, leading me to believe she was waiting for someone too. I saw her eyes narrow as the door banged open, and a gaggle of girls from the bank walked in.

Rita Matthews led the group towards the bar and loudly called for drinks all around. I watched as she held court over the other girls. She was obviously the alpha in the teller crew. Glancing back over my shoulder, I noticed the girl at the table behind me was glaring at Rita with undisguised hatred. I needed to see what was going on there. Besides, it'd be better to let Rita get a few drinks in her before I approached her, right?

I grabbed my drink and sat down beside the girl, not bothering to ask if it was ok. She was so hyper-focused on Rita, I don't think she even noticed I was there.

"Hey, I couldn't help but notice you looking over at the girl there. Do you know her?"

She startled and turned to me, cocking her head.

"Do I know you?"

64

"No, I was sitting over there and thought you looked lonely. I'm Hannah Murphy. I'm a reporter with the Post. What's up with the redhead?"

She seemed hesitant to answer until Rita let loose with a peal of laughter that rang through the bar. With a roll of her eyes, she turned back and focused on me.

"Hi Hannah, I'm Lanie Edwards. I used to work at the bank until that slut stole my job and my man."

Oh, this was interesting. I leaned in closer, sensing this girl was going to be more than willing to talk.

"That sucks. What happened?"

She played with a hank of her slightly greasy hair and focused on her split ends. She wasn't unattractive but compared with the vibrant Rita, she looked like she was the type to fade into the background.

"Well, I was dating this amazing man, Mark Brown. I still can't believe he's gone," she said with a sniff. "We were so happy, and then she got hired. I didn't stand a chance. Once she was there, he didn't even know I existed. Three days later, he dumped me."

"I'm sorry, Lanie. That must have been really hard. You said something about her taking your job, too?"

"Yeah, it wasn't enough she took my man. She noticed I made a mistake on my drawer and reported me. I got fired, I still can't find a job, and it's all her fault. And she probably is the one who killed poor Mark!"

She dropped her hair and clenched her fists. If looks could have killed, poor Rita would be dead at the bar.

"Wow, that's a run of horrible luck. I'm doing a story on Mark's life. Would it be ok if I asked you a few questions?"

That got her attention back on me.

"If I do, will she get arrested? Ooh, maybe she could get the death penalty."

Ouch, this girl had it in for Rita. I could see being mad about losing your job, but losing Mark really didn't seem like it was a massive loss from what other people had said about him. I didn't know what to say at first and finally sputtered the first thing that came to mind.

"Um, well, I guess if she killed him, she would be. What do you know?"

Lanie leaned towards me, eyes gleaming with unbalanced hope. Oh boy, this was going to be interesting.

She talked for about fifteen minutes, going over every perceived slight in exact detail. From the sounds of it, she'd been stalking both Rita and Mark after the breakup, and I wouldn't have been at all shocked to learn she had pictures of both of them plastering her walls at home. While I heard a lot about their romance and how perfect Mark was, I heard nothing that would lead me to believe Rita had killed him. I tried to hang in there and look interested, but I was drifting.

"And she got me fired for being off a couple of bucks in my drawer, while never saying a word about Mark's 'commissions,'" she said, finally running out of steam.

That grabbed my attention right back from where it had wandered.

"Wait, what? What do you mean by commissions? Isn't that part of how the bank pays its lenders?"

She looked at me with a slow smile.

"That's not how it works at all. See, the lender gets paid a set salary, and then they have benchmarks they need to hit. Once they get to certain levels, they get bonuses, but there are never any commissions. I noticed Mark was buying a ton of new clothes, expensive watches, and looking at a new Range Rover. When I asked him about it, he said he was getting some good commission money, but I knew that's not how it worked."

"When did this start?"

"Right before we broke up, so about two months ago, I think."

Wow, if she was this intense two months after a breakup, I couldn't imagine what she'd been like right after it happened.

"Do you have any proof of what he was doing?"

She grimaced and took a sip of her drink.

"No, he never got me anything. But you see those earrings Rita's wearing? They're real diamonds. He gave them to her about a week before he died. I still can't believe he's gone. We were gonna get back together, you know? The earrings were a parting gift. I could feel it. He was ready to come back to me. She might have lured him away with her flashy looks, but I was the one who loved him."

She brushed a tear away from her eyes before turning to glare at Rita again. I wasn't sure if I could believe a word she'd said, but she'd given me some interesting leads to chase. Time to talk to Rita.

"Well, thanks for your time, Lanie. I appreciate it."

"Can I have your card? I might think of something else that would help."

The last thing I wanted to do was give her my card, but I handed it over against my better judgment. You never knew where your next big tip could come from. I just hoped the tip didn't come with a lock of Rita's hair.

"Lanie, you know, it might be better to move on and try something different. It can't be good to come here and be reminded of everything you lost. Maybe focus on the future and see what's ahead?"

She whipped her head back around and glared at me.

"I will never be over Mark. You have no idea what he meant to me. I won't rest until she pays for what she did!"

All right then, that's what I got for handing out unsolicited advice, right? I put up my hands and backed away.

"Sorry, just trying to help. Have a good night!"

She didn't answer, she was too preoccupied with glaring at the back of Rita's head. I wandered up to the bar where the girls were sitting and waved to the bartender for a refill. I turned to Rita and tried to start up a conversation.

"Hey, you work over at First Legacy, right?" I asked. Hopefully, she hadn't noticed me talking to the woman currently glaring holes in the back of her head.

Rita's eyes were unfocused as she turned to face me. She blinked hard and addressed her answer slightly to the left of where I was standing.

"Yeah, I work there. Who wants to know?"

"I'm Hannah Murphy. I work for the Post."

"Like, a fence post?"

Oh, dear. This wouldn't be as easy as I thought.

"No, I'm a reporter for a newspaper."

She giggled and blew a raspberry before answering my right shoulder.

"Silly me, a fence post. That's funny. Whatcha want?"

"I just had a few questions about Mark Brown. I'm writing a story about him."

She sobered up slightly and finally met my eyes. Her big brown eyes filled with tears, and she bit her top lip before she answered.

"I miss him so much. He was going to buy me a necklace to match these earrings. See these earrings? Anyway, I was supposed to get the necklace this week, but then he died, and I got nothing!"

She started bawling, and I glanced at the girls she was with, hoping one of them would serve as backup. As one, the group scuttled down the bar. I was on my own.

"I'm sorry. You're Rita, right?"

She hiccuped and nodded her head.

"Yeah, I was dating Mark. He bought me lots of jewelry. I miss that. We met at the bank. I'm a teller there, but I'm supposed to be moving up. Mark promised me."

"What did he promise you?"

Her tears miraculously dried up, and she tilted her head as she answered.

"He said if I was a good girl and kept quiet, he'd make sure I got ahead. That's the only reason I stayed there. My boss is a creep who won't stop looking up my skirt and down my shirt. Haha, up my skirt and down my shirt."

Wow, this girl was white-girl-wasted already, and she'd only been in the bar for half an hour. I seriously hoped she'd get a ride home.

"Do you mean Gerald Harms?"

"Yeah, Harmie. I guess he's not so bad, but I dunno, I wanna be more than a teller, you know? I wanna get more money. Mark said he was onto something big, but he never let me know what."

"Do you know Lanie Edwards?"

Rita snorted and ended up inhaling her drink. She sputtered and coughed right on my shirt. Lovely.

"That loser? How can I not know her? She stalks me everywhere, sitting at the same table every time I come in here and glaring at me. They never dated, you know? I saw you talking to her. Whatever she said, it's a lie. He wouldn't date a mousy thing like her. She was stalking him before she switched to me."

She signaled the bartender for another round, nearly tipping over as she waved her hand.

"Rita, maybe some water would be better?"

"Don't tell me how to live my life! I lost the best thing that ever happened to me. I need to drown my sorrows."

"Mark meant a lot to you, huh?"

"Mark? Oh yeah, him too. I meant the necklace, though. That would have set me up for life. It was so sparkly. Why did he have to die before he bought it?"

The bartender slid her drink over, and she downed half of it before looking at me blearily.

"Do you have a ride home?" I asked.

"Don't worry about me, girly. I always find a way."

And with that, I'd had enough of the First Legacy crew. What a day! I made sure I had everything in my bag and headed out the front door, ramming into someone who was coming in.

"Again? I'm going to need a chest protector if you keep slamming into me. For such a little thing, you pack quite a wallop," Ben said.

Darn it. Why did I keep running into this guy?

"Sorry, I need to look where I'm going. I'm just heading home."

"Learn anything interesting from the teller crew?"

"Ha, only that you probably need to watch Lanie before she hunts Rita down and steals her skin. Seriously, she gives off some junior serial killer vibes. The only crime Rita committed was ruining my shirt," I said, looking down at the wet spots on my tee.

He fell in beside me as we walked around the corner to the parking lot.

"Well, you just saved me some time. I was planning on eavesdropping and seeing if any of them were willing to talk."

"Well, if you want to talk to them, I'd wait for Rita to sober up."

As I walked to the driver's side of my Blazer, I felt something crunch beneath my feet. I peered through the dark, trying to see what I was walking on. Ben put a hand on my arm.

"Hannah, stop, that's glass."

He held up his phone and used his flashlight to light up the side of my car. Sure enough, the driver's side window was broken. Son of a biscuit! I didn't need this.

"Oh no, not my window. That's going to be so expensive," I said as I reached for the handle.

"Wait, there's something on your seat."

He reached through the broken window and lifted out a note, holding onto it by a corner. As he shone his light on it, I could read what it said.

If you know what's good for you, you'll leave this story alone.

Even though it was a pleasant night, I couldn't stop my teeth from chattering. I looked up into Ben's eyes and tried to stop my legs from shaking.

CHAPTER 9

*B*y the time Ben called the department and had my poor Blazer processed for prints, it was way past my bedtime. He offered to follow me home, and I was too tired to argue. As we walked up the steps, I remembered the carrier I'd bought for Razzy. I'd forgotten to check to see if it was still in the back. I mumbled to Ben I'd be right back and jogged down the step.

Luckily, it was still there! I grabbed the bag and trudged back up the steps, completely ready for this day to be over. Ben was waiting outside my door with a smile on his face.

"New gift for your cat?"

"Yeah, I need to get her out more. I feel bad she's cooped up in here all day."

"I'd do the same for Gus, but he's one big cat. I don't know if I could find a carrier large enough for him."

I opened the door and flipped on the light in my apartment in time to see Razzy jogging through the hall towards me.

"Mama! Where have you been? Why do I smell fear? Oh, you brought the cute detective home."

She wound her way around my legs, sniffing loudly while carrying on a running commentary.

"Your cat's sure happy to see you. She's so talkative," Ben said, leaning against the doorjamb.

"Yeah, she does that," I said, feeling terrible I wasn't answering her.

She seemed to understand and sat at Ben's feet, gazing up at him. He leaned down to pet her on the head, and she arched up into his hand. What a little minx! I could tell Ben was enamored with her as she blinked her pretty blue eyes at him. My cat had better game than I did.

"So, you'll be ok here tonight?" Ben asked, scratching Razzy under the chin.

"Yeah, I'll be fine. Thanks for seeing me home."

"I'll let you know if I find out who broke out your window. If you need a good garage, I can text you the one I use. Your insurance should cover it."

"That would be great. My cell number is on my card."

The level of awkwardness ratcheted up as we both stood there. I wasn't sure what to say, and Ben looked like he didn't either. He finally ran his hand through his close-cropped hair and moved towards the door.

"Well, have a good night. Stay safe. Let me know if you need anything."

"Will do," I said as I closed the door behind him.

"Mama! You should have offered him something to drink," Razzy said, lashing her tail. "That was just rude."

I leaned up against the door and waited a few minutes to make sure Ben was gone before I answered her.

"Sorry, Razzy, it's been a long night. Besides, he's a professional, and he was just seeing me home. I don't want him to get the wrong idea."

Ok, maybe I wouldn't have minded all that much if he got the wrong idea, but I sure wouldn't tell my cat that!

"What happened? I still smell fear on you," Razzy said, her little nostrils delicately flaring. "And what's in the bag?"

I relayed what happened in the bar and to my car as she listened raptly. As I talked, I remembered I hadn't eaten yet. Razzy followed me into the kitchen as I poured a bowl of cereal and added some milk. Dinner of champions, or something like that, I thought as I dug in the drawer for a spoon. More like dinner for people who are too tired to cook and don't feel like ordering takeout.

Razzy listened intently, her eyes going round as I got to the part about my window.

"You could have been hurt. If I'd been there, I would have slashed them!"

Her claws flashed at the end of her little mittens before retracting again. While I admired her courage, it made me think about what I'd do if someone tried to hurt my little girl.

"I'm glad you weren't there, you really could have been hurt," I said, in between bites of cereal. "I'm not so sure I should take you along with me now. What if this happens again? I couldn't take it if anything happened to you."

Her ears flattened, and her pupils dilated as she glared up at me.

"I think I know how to handle myself. Thank you very much. I could find my way home from anywhere. If someone came at me, I'd slash and run. I'm not an idiot."

"Sorry, sorry. I just worry about you."

I rinsed out my bowl and put it in the dishwasher before grabbing the bag I brought home from the pet store. I made a ceremony out of the big reveal while Razzy watched. She walked around the bag, sniffing intently before sitting next to it.

"I like it. This will work nicely. Now I'll be able to come with you and help solve this crime. No offense, but humans lack subtlety. With the two of us working together, we'll figure this out in no time. Maybe you'll even get a reward! Ooh, or maybe you'll win a Pulitzer for your story. We could be the toast of the town."

"I'd settle for an ongoing position as a feature writer and some money in the bank if it's all the same to you. Now, let me tell you about the people I interviewed today."

We moved over to the couch, and I turned on the television softly in the background as I filled Razzy in on each person I'd interviewed. She listened and offered her insights into each person.

"My money's on the crazy girl, Lanie, or the banker dude," Razzy said, licking her paw and scrubbing it around her ear. "There's something off about him."

"Yeah, I feel you. We'll see. I'm going to see if I can track down the last person on the list, Tim Waters, at the gym tomorrow. He never answered my message asking for an interview, but hopefully I can catch him there. I can't take you with me, but I'll come home and take you to work with me. I hope you'll be comfy in there. It doesn't have much room for you to turn around."

"I'll make it work. I can't wait for the morning, my first real adventure!"

I smiled as she went through her bathing routine before settling on the couch next to me to sleep. I watched television for a bit before my eyes got too heavy to keep open. Scooping up Razzy, I headed for bed, ready to put this day behind me.

* * *

WHEN MY ALARM went off a few hours later, I groaned, wondering why on earth I wanted to track someone down at a gym this early. Who in their right mind worked out at five in the morning?

I got dressed in a pair of yoga pants and an old tee while I waited for my coffee to brew. Razzy was still snuggled in bed, but she cracked an eye open as I made the bed.

"Keep it down, would you? Why are you up so early?"

"I have to meet that guy at the gym, remember? I'll be back in a little while."

She closed her eyes and huffed a sigh. I shrugged and walked into the kitchen to get my travel mug ready. With any luck, I'd be back here in less than an hour. I pulled up the address for the gym as I walked out to my car, grimacing as I remembered my broken window. It would be a chilly ride this morning, but with any luck, it would help me wake up.

When I got to the gym, I had to fend off an overly enthusiastic gym bunny at the front desk who was intent on selling me a year's membership. While I loved hiking, I wasn't one for the gym. After the third try, she finally agreed to sell me a day pass. I stowed my bag in the women's locker room and wandered through the weight room, trying to spot Tim Waters. I'd seen his social media pictures from the gym, and it looked like this was the time he was usually there.

Just when I thought I would strikeout, he came around the corner with a towel thrown over his shoulder. He was dripping with sweat and holding a racquetball paddle, leading me to guess he'd just finished playing. Look at me with my brilliant deductions!

I figured the best way to start up a conversation was to ask him a question about one of the weight machines and hope he'd be talkative. As he approached, I stepped in his path and put on my biggest smile.

"Hi, I'm sorry, but do you know how to operate this machine?"

He looked at me and then looked at the machine. Dang it, I'd picked one of the simplest devices there.

"Well, miss, that's the seated overhead press. You sit there and push the bar up and let it come back down. Here, I'll show you."

Whew! Leave it to a man to want to give me a full explanation of how a piece of gym equipment worked. For once, mansplaining was benefiting me.

He sat down and patiently showed me how it all worked. He was a nice-looking guy, with brown hair and blue eyes. He didn't give off the same vibe as Wesley had, leaving me wondering how he'd been friends with Mark. After a few reps, he offered to spot me and correct my form on the machine.

I diligently tried to look as though I was super into working out as he monitored my progress.

"So, I'm guessing you play racquetball?" I asked.

"Yep, just finished. My old partner died, so it was just me today," Tim said. "Do you play?"

"No, but I thought I'd recognized you from some of Mark Brown's posts. I was friends with him on Instagram," I said, hoping he'd never check Mark's friend list and find out I was lying. "It's crazy that he's gone."

Tim sat on the bench next to me and wiped his face with his towel.

"Yeah, he was a good dude. I'll miss him."

"Did you know him well?"

"We were friends for probably eight years, I think. I met him in college. He went into banking, and I went into the tech sector, so we didn't see each other often. I'm not really into the party scene, but we still liked to meet up to play a little ball here. Did you know him well? I don't think I've ever seen you before. Trust me. I would've remembered you."

He gave me a genuine smile, and I couldn't help but like this guy. He wasn't like the rest of Mark's crowd. I mentally crossed him off my list.

"I wasn't that close, just a friend of a friend kind of thing," I said.

"I see, well, looks like you've got this machine down. I've gotta go clean up, but maybe I'll see you around?"

"Sure, thanks for the help."

There was no way I was going to tell him my arms were burning with the heat of a thousand suns from the reps I'd been doing while we talked. This undercover stuff was exhausting! My arms were going to be limp noodles for the rest of the day. I waited for him to disappear before packing it up and hurrying back out to my car.

Once I got home, I got cleaned up, wincing as I tried to dry my hair with the blow dryer. I felt muscles I hadn't used in years since I was back on the farm. Maybe I really should join a gym.

By the time I was ready for work, Razzy had used her litter box and pronounced herself willing to travel. She delicately stepped into the carrier, turned around, and made herself comfortable. I slipped my laptop and notebook in the back and got ready to slide the straps over my shoulders. The contraption was too awkward to get over one shoulder, and I didn't want to drop her, so I placed the bag on the table and lined up the straps. Maybe I could slip them on, one at a time, and then it wouldn't feel as heavy.

"Holy crap, cat, how much do you weigh?" I asked, struggling my way into the straps.

"Hey, that's rude! I never ask how much you weigh."

"And you never have to carry me. I don't know why you feel so much heavier than you do when I pick you up."

"It's probably your laptop," Razzy said with a sniff.

I finally got everything sorted out and walked through the door, trying not to pitch forward. Between my workout at the gym and lugging Razzy around all day, I'd be lucky to have use of my arms tomorrow.

"Slow it down, would you? I'm getting motion sickness," Razzy said, with a piteous little meow.

"Sorry, we'll get this figured out. It will be worth it, right?"

"I'm not so sure now. There's so much noise out here."

I slid the straps off my shoulders and placed the bag on the ground to open up the back door. I noticed the top strap on the bag and figured I'd use that for the time being. I could always switch arms if one got tired.

As I drove to the paper, I looked in the rearview mirror to see how Razzy was doing. Her eyes were wide as she took in the sights of vehicles rushing past. She had a little smile on her face, and it made me happy. I could only imagine what she was going to think of my colleagues. Or what they were going to think of her! With any luck, I could stash her in my cubicle, and no one would know the difference.

CHAPTER 10

Wednesday, June 24th

$\mathcal{A}$s I walked into the newsroom, I felt immediately at home in the chaos. There was something so invigorating about the sound of reporters tapping frantically on their keyboards, trying to distill the day's news into what people wanted to know. I walked to my cubicle, sliding Razzy's bag under my desk after I grabbed my laptop.

I cracked it open and looked over my day's assignments. Tom had posted a note wanting an update on the Mark Brown story, and I had a few small stories I'd need to finish before the end of the day. After making a few notes on what I'd need to research for those, I swung my chair around, ready to head to Tom's office.

Unfortunately, at that same moment, Vinnie stopped by. I sank back in my chair and prayed for patience. One of these days, the prayers were going to work, right? Anybody?

"Hey, good lookin, what're you up to today? Saw your story on the jewelry store. Now that's more your style. I'm glad you handed over your piece on the murder," Vinnie said, using a toothpick to dig between his teeth as he spoke.

Yes, that was about as appealing as it sounds. I shuddered and didn't miss the tiny huffing sound under my desk. I nudged Razzy's bag with my foot to remind her to stay quiet.

"I'm not sure what you mean, Vinnie. I'm still working on that story. The jewelry store was an extra piece."

His face folded into a frown as my words sunk in. He twitched his nose and rubbed at it, apparently forgetting he still had the toothpick. He narrowly missed impaling his nose.

"Hmph. I need to talk to Tom about it, I guess. I don't know what our paper is coming to, giving prime stories like that to little girls like you. It needs a man's touch. You'll probably write some weepy story about his personal life instead of doing the legwork to figure out who's guilty."

His nose continued to twitch, and his eyes were turning red. I cocked my head, wondering what was wrong as he let out an explosive sneeze.

"Vinnie, are you ok? I mean, I'm kinda used to the misogyny, but it rarely comes with a side of snot."

"I'm fine," he said, sounding all plugged up. "My allergies are acting up, I guess. Anyway, I need to go see Tom."

"You do that," I said, swinging back around to my laptop.

I attacked my keyboard viciously, ready to do someone serious harm. Vinnie's comments usually rolled right off my back, but that one hurt. I was more determined than ever to sort out this murder. My visit with Tom was going to wait.

I pulled up my browser and thought about where I wanted to start. So far, I'd interviewed everyone on the list Jolie had given me. I switched over to my word processor and typed up my general thoughts, hoping the exercise would clear up what I'd learned and reveal something I'd missed.

After a few minutes of distilling everything I'd learned, a knock on my cubicle startled me. I whipped my head around and was relieved to see Ashley standing there. She looked refreshed, so I wondered if she'd moved on from the energizer bunny.

"Hey, Ash! It's good to see you. I've missed our chats. I've been so busy chasing this story, I haven't been here much. What's up with you?"

She walked in and leaned against my filing cabinet.

"Oh girl, you have no idea what you've missed. You know Pat, the one who works sports? Well, you'll never believe what happened last night!"

Ashley filled me in on all the office gossip I'd missed, and I laughed, feeling a lot lighter than I had when Vinnie left. Once she'd run out of steam, I bounced a few ideas off of her.

"So, Ash, this story I'm working on. I'm kind of stuck. I was working the angle of who Mark Brown was as a person, and I've learned a bunch of different things."

"Hit me. We'll figure it out together."

I grabbed my notebook out of the bag, not missing how Ashley looked down and saw Razzy. She smiled and shook her head. I held my finger up to my lips, and she winked before rolling her eyes.

As I went through my list of suspects with her, she nodded along and asked a few questions. Once I was finished, she held up six fingers.

"Ok, so the nice guy, Tim, cross him off your list. Ditto with Jordan and Rita. Jordan doesn't have a motive, and Rita wouldn't have killed her cash cow. That leaves you with three people, plus maybe the irate boss or even a client."

"Maybe you're right. I'm probably overthinking it, but I feel like I'm missing something important. Thanks, Ash. You're the best!"

She patted me on the shoulder and headed back to her cubicle.

"Just remember that the next time I need a favor."

I peeked under my desk, smiling at Razzy. She was sitting up, looking at me intently. I almost asked her for her thoughts when my phone rang. I looked at the screen and saw it was Georgia North.

"Hi, Georgia," I said, answering it before it could go to voicemail.

"Hi, you know how you wanted me to look through some of Mark's files? I think I found something."

I sat up straight in my chair, excited to hear what she had to say next.

"Do you want to tell me over the phone?"

"No, I need to meet you somewhere. I can get away in about fifteen minutes. Can you meet me at the Roasted Bean? It's right by the bank."

"I'll be there."

I ended the call and grabbed Razzy's bag. I stuffed everything in the back pocket and headed out of my cubicle. Luckily, everyone was intent on their work and didn't notice me lugging the bag out of there. As I got to my car, my open window reminded me I needed to get it fixed. I made a mental note to do that after I met Georgia.

Once I got to the coffee shop, I picked a table outside so I could bring Razzy with me. I ordered a cup of cappuccino and a pastry while I waited. After I broke off a small piece to share with Razzy, she thanked me quietly. Her eyes were wide as she took in the traffic noise and the bustle of the busy coffee shop patio.

"Hannah, thanks for meeting me," Georgia said, bustling up to the table.

She had a file folder in her hand, and she looked around before she sat across from me.

"Thanks for coming. I'm looking forward to what you found."

"Well, it's pretty significant. In fact, I should probably turn this over to the bank and not a reporter, but I don't think they'd do anything about it. I think Harms may be in on it."

Now I was thoroughly intrigued. I listened as she opened the folder and explained what she found. Some financial stuff was way over my head, but by the time she was done talking, I think I had a good grasp of it all.

"So, you're saying Mark was embezzling small amounts from all of his clients? Nothing too much, just a little every month. Why do you think Harms is involved?" I asked.

"Well, I pulled up their accounts last night after work. I noticed each of them had deposits that couldn't be accounted for without that explanation. I think Harms knew what Mark was doing and wanted in on the action," she said, closing the file folder and sliding it over to me. "I made you a copy of everything."

"Wow, I appreciate this. Do you have a problem if I share this with the police?"

Her eyes darted around, and her neck reddened.

"I guess that's fine. Just, please, keep my name out of it."

"I will. Let me know if you find anything else out? I noticed Wesley Laughlin has a blue binder I saw in Mark's office before. Do you think you could get a look at that?"

"That's Mark's book of clients. I can try but Wesley, the little worm, usually has it on him at all times."

"Well, if you can, that'd be great. There may be some good information in there."

"I will. I've got to get back. Thanks again," she said, sliding her chair back.

I opened up the folders and heard Razzy's soft voice from under the table.

"Mama, that lady wasn't telling you the whole truth."

I looked around and acted like I was tying my shoe to answer her without looking like a crazy person.

"What do you mean, Razzy?"

"I could tell she was keeping something back. I don't know what it is, but she smelled like she was lying."

"You can smell lies?"

She huffed and fluffed up her fur, turning around. I was going to need to get her out of the cramped bag and back home so she could stretch out.

"It's not that I smell lies. It's just human scents change when they tell lies. That's why I like you so much. You're always honest with me."

"Well, thanks. I need to call Ben, and then I'll take you home, ok?"

She nodded and I straightened back up, bonking my head on the table. I rubbed the sore spot and looked around. So far, no one seemed to look my way, so I hoped I hadn't been seen having an in-depth conversation with my bag.

I pulled out my phone and dialed Ben's number. He answered on the second ring.

"Hannah, what's up?"

"Hey, Ben. You're never going to believe what I found out. Do you have time to meet me later?"

"I'm gonna be tied up for the next few hours. Do you want to have dinner or something, and you can tell me then?"

I paused, unsure of how to answer. Was this like a date? My palms started sweating. Why did he have to be so handsome?

"Um, sure, I guess," I said, stammering and feeling like a complete idiot. "Where would you like to meet?"

"You know the Greek place that's about three blocks from your apartment?"

"Yeah, Santorini's?"

"That's the one. Let's meet up there at six."

"Ok, see you then."

I wasn't sure how to process my feelings about meeting with Ben for dinner. I'm sure he just wanted to kill two birds with one stone, right? I mean, this wasn't like a date or anything. It was just about the case.

I rubbed my palms on my jeans and stood up, desperate for physical activity to keep my mind busy. I was going to go for an Olympic medal in overthinking if I wasn't careful. I grabbed Razzy's bag, deciding to head home and drop her off before I got my window fixed.

As I drove home, my phone rang again. I answered it without looking.

"Hannah! Where are you?" Tom asked, his usually gravely voice sounding madder than usual.

"I'm driving right now. I need to get my window fixed. Why, what's up?"

"Have you seen the piece Dave Freidrich did in today's Times?"

"No, I haven't. What's wrong?"

"Pull over, read it and get back to me," he said, hanging up his desk phone with a bang.

Well, that didn't sound good. Since I was almost home, I drove on, parked, and ran up the stairs. I unzipped Razzy's bag, and she stretched as I opened up my laptop. She jumped up on the table next to me as the website for the Times loaded.

"Mama, he sounded furious."

"Yeah, I guess we'll find out why shortly."

I scanned through the piece, feeling angrier at every line I read. That rat! He claimed to have inside information and accused the local police force of covering up the real story. Ben, in particular, was portrayed as unflatteringly as possible. I took a deep breath and called Tom.

"It's me. I just read it. What is he thinking?"

"Have you found anything like that in your research?" Tom asked, barking out each word.

"No, but I have found something that could blow this case wide open. I'll know more tonight, and I'll have my story ready before the deadline for tomorrow's issue."

"You better. I'm putting a lot of trust in you. Dave's story makes us look like we're missing the boat here, and I don't like it. You need to get this moving!"

I winced as Tom slammed his phone down again. Razzy rubbed her head against my cheek and purred a little.

"Don't let him get to you. You've got this," Razzy said, sitting back down and looking at me earnestly.

"I hope so, Razzy. I need to go over what Georgia gave me and then figure out if she's lying about something."

"Trust me. She's lying."

I patted her on the head and got ready to leave again. I'd get my window fixed in between now and meeting Ben. Luckily, Tom's call had my stomach already worked into knots, making me forget about my nervousness over dinner. Almost.

CHAPTER 11

Santorini's interior design made you feel as if you'd escaped to the Greek isles, and I've always loved it. There was something so cheerful about the stark white tables and bright blue linens offset with little candles. As I walked in, I saw Ben had already been seated at a booth. I clamped down on my nervousness and forced myself to smile.

I'd taken a little time to change clothes after getting my window fixed. What? I knew it wasn't a date, but this guy was gorgeous! The host seated me across from Ben and slid a menu in front of me.

"Thanks for meeting me here," Ben said. "I missed lunch, and food has been the only thing on my mind. By the time I got out of my meeting with the chief, I barely had time to make it here."

"I'm guessing the meeting had to do with that hit piece in the Times?"

"For sure," he said, scrubbing his hands on the side of his head. "I'm not sure where he got his information, but most of it's wrong. You can't ever trust a reporter."

I swallowed hard and tried not to let my disappointment show. Ben noticed my reaction and smiled.

"Present company excluded. You've been honest with me and fair in your coverage. So far, anyway. It just always feels like reporters and cops are at odds, and we usually are, truth be told."

"I think it's better to work as a team," I said, tracing the condensation on my glass with my finger. "We're all working towards the same goal. I don't think it's necessary to be adversaries."

"Well, if the rest of your colleagues could be like that, it would be just fine with me."

Our server arrived to take our orders. I hadn't even cracked the menu since I already knew what I wanted. You could never go wrong with a Greek salad piled high with feta cheese. I'd discovered this place when I first moved here in college, and it had quickly become a favorite.

Ben ordered the souvlaki with a side of pita bread, reminding me it never hurt to get extra pita. I asked for some too before our server left.

"So, I heard from a source today, and I'm sorry, but I can't share their name. They passed along some interesting information. Once I saw it, I knew I had to go to you. This is way over my head and possibly super illegal."

"Tell me more," Ben said, leaning closer to me.

I pulled the file out of my bag and slid it across the table.

"So, it looks like, according to these documents, Mark Brown was embezzling small amounts from his clients. Alone, they aren't much, but across the board and with how often it occurred, it's actually a big amount of money."

Ben opened the folders and started going through the columns. He looked thoughtful, and I couldn't help but stare at the way he bit his lip while he read.

"Interesting. What else did your source have?"

"They think the bank manager, Gerald Harms, is involved too. Apparently, they found similar deposits that went into his personal account. The only thing is, Razzy says my source is lying, and I don't know what they're lying about."

I realized my error as soon as it came out and slammed my mouth shut. Maybe he hadn't been listening?

"Did you just say your cat said your source was lying?"

"Um, no, well, it's just been a long day. What I meant was I have a feeling my source isn't telling me everything."

I'm not good under pressure, as you can see. That was probably the lamest excuse I've ever come up with, and I seriously doubted he was going to buy it. Ben cocked an eyebrow at me, but I was saved from answering by our server arriving with our food. That was close. I needed to be careful. We both tore into our food. I used my pita bread to mop up the extra dressing, and only sheer willpower kept me from groaning aloud at how amazing it was.

Once we were done with our food, Ben opened the file folder again and continued looking at the pages.

"Thanks for bringing me this. I'll have our forensic accountant team go through it and see what they have to say. I assume you're ready to release some of this in your next column?"

"I thought I'd wait to see if you minded. I don't want to jeopardize your case," I said.

He snorted and gave a sarcastic laugh. "That's probably the first time that's ever been said to me."

"Well, I care. I want to find out who killed this guy. I was the one who discovered his body, and I feel like it needs to be done the right way. If you're ok with it, I'll float a bit of information in my piece that will publish tomorrow and see if we get a reaction out of the bank."

"Let's do it. I'm curious to see what will happen."

I played with my napkin, folding it into various shapes as I thought about my next question. I didn't want to alienate Ben, but I wanted to know more about why he came here. His old department was much bigger and had a lot more opportunities for advancement. And maybe a little part of me wanted to know if he planned on hanging around town for a while.

"If you don't mind me asking, what brought you to Golden Hills?"

"I don't mind at all. I worked as a detective in Sacramento. That's where I'm from. A few things happened, and I decided I needed a change of pace. I like it here so far. It's got the big city amenities without the crazy big city feel to it. I need to get out more and enjoy the scenery, though. I miss hiking."

"Oh, you like to hike, too? I love it, especially around here. There are so many hikes. It would take a lifetime to complete them all. Maybe sometime you'd like to come with me?"

I felt the heatwave of shame scorch across my face as I realized what I'd just said. I looked down at my napkin and smoothed it flat. I felt a touch on my hand and looked up to see him smiling, his green eyes brightening. The little crinkles that formed at the corners of his eyes were so cute.

"I'd love that, Hannah. Maybe we could do it on Saturday morning?"

"Great! That would be cool. So, what made you pick this town?"

"I wanted to stay in policing, and there were quite a few jobs out there. I'd always heard good things about this area and wanted to check it out. I didn't know anyone, which was a big plus. I needed to get away and start fresh."

There was a story there, but I could sense Ben wasn't quite ready to share it with me yet. It went against my nature to avoid prying, but from the look in his eyes, the reason behind his leaving was a painful one. I could wait until he was ready to tell me. That reminded me of Josh with the Trib. He seemed to want to dig into Ben's background. Once again, I hoped he wouldn't find anything bad. I liked Ben a lot, and it would suck if it turned out he wasn't a good person. Fine, yes, I'll admit I liked him.

My gut told me he was ok. Razzy liked him, and for me, that was enough for now.

"Hopefully, you like it here. It gets pretty hot in the summer, but it's nice in the winter. We get snow, but it never gets super cold. Or at least, not very often."

"I can't wait for winter. I always felt like I was missing out in California."

"Wait to say that until you experience your first week of winter driving," I said, laughing. "You might just change your mind."

"Very true, I haven't experienced a full winter here yet. Based on your articles, it seems like you've interviewed quite a few of the people who knew Mark. What are your impressions so far?"

I was flattered Ben was interested in what I'd learned. I told him about the people on my list, being careful not to mention Georgia as my source. I went through what Ashley and I'd discussed regarding possible motives and who we thought might have done it.

"Good work, you've accomplished a lot. Maybe you should have been a detective instead of a reporter."

"Thanks," I said, blushing at the compliment. "Is there anything you can share about what you've learned? Off the record, of course."

He held up his fingers and started ticking off each person.

"Jordan has an alibi for that night. She was at an event during the time leading up to and after you discovered Mark's body. Georgia North was home alone, and so far, we can't corroborate that. Wesley worked late, and no one saw him, so he's still in the running. Gerald Harms was home with his wife. Rita was at the bar and stayed after Mark left. Lanie was at the same bar until after Rita left, and Tim was at a different event during those hours."

"So, we're left with Georgia, Wesley, and a potential client who found out about the embezzlement. Actually, I'd keep Harms on the list, too."

"Really? Why?"

"Just a gut feeling. A lot is going on with him, and it looks like he might have been embezzling too. Maybe Mark threatened to turn him in. I think he was having an affair with Harms' wife, but I can't prove it yet."

"Interesting. Those are the people I've been focusing on, but I'll look deeper into Harms. Oh, did you get your window fixed? I'm still waiting for a match on the prints. It's a long shot. I'm assuming whoever did it wore gloves."

"I got it fixed, thanks. I can't say I've ever been threatened over a story before, but then again, I usually write about store openings and community events. Not much to cause someone to break windows over those subjects."

"Well, be careful. There's a chance that whoever broke it is involved in this case. Do you want me to follow you home again?"

"No, it's ok. You've had a long day. I'll be fine. I've got to get home and file my story. I'll let you know what I hear on my end. I have a feeling I'm about to poke the bear with a stick, but hopefully, it'll be worth it."

I slid out of the booth, and Ben followed me up to the front to pay. I pulled out my wallet and stopped when I felt his hand on mine again. He had such warm hands.

"I've got this, Hannah. It was nice to have dinner with you. Maybe we can do it again sometime?"

"That'd be great."

I felt my heart zip a little faster in my chest and wished I could be more eloquent with my words. Pouring my heart out on paper was easy, but getting those words from my brain to my tongue usually resulted in a traffic jam and then a nasty pile-up along the way.

Ben walked me to my car, and we stood there awkwardly. I knew I needed to get home, but I didn't want to leave his company.

"Well, thanks again," Ben said, clearing his throat. "I had a nice time."

"I did, too. Good night."

I climbed in my Blazer and waved as I pulled out of the parking lot, excited to get home and tell Razzy all about my evening. As I drove, I started putting together the outline of my story. I needed to be careful with how I worded the accusation of embezzlement, particularly with Harms.

Razzy was sitting in front of the door when I got home, and she blinked as I flipped on the light.

"Oh, sorry, I didn't mean to hurt your eyes," I said, reaching to pet her head.

She gave me a head bump on the leg before marching in place as I petted her.

"It's fine. I'm used to it. It just takes a second for my eyes to adjust. You smell like Greek food. Did you bring me any?"

"No, sweetie, sorry. I just had a salad, and I don't think you'd like lettuce."

"I might. I'm open-minded."

"Well, I'll remember that next time."

I put my bag on the kitchen table and flipped open my laptop. As I waited for it to load, I grabbed a can of Razzy's food and dished it up for her. Remembering she wanted to eat at the table now, I moved my laptop and placed her bowl in front of the other chair. She hopped up, purring, and dug in noisily.

I smiled and shook my head as I started typing up my story. The words came quickly and before I knew it, I had a finished piece ready to go. I took a deep breath and hit enter, sending my story through the portal. It would go through editorial first, and then it would be on the website before getting printed in the morning edition. I wondered how long it would take to get some nibbles from the bank about what I'd said.

I closed my laptop and admired Razzy as she cleaned up after eating her meal. Her delicate little paws swished around her face, pausing up at her ear before going back down towards her whiskers.

"Ok, now that I'm done cleaning up, I want to hear all about your dinner," Razzy said.

I picked her up and settled down on the couch, holding her close. She gave a little coo as I mentioned Ben wanted to hike with me. Her eyes got all wide, and she patted my arm.

"What?" I asked.

"You could get me a harness, and I could come, too! I've heard about adventure cats. There's that dog and cat right here in Colorado who are famous! I want to be an adventure cat, too!"

"Um, well, you might not like it. A hike can take a few hours, and you'd get tired pretty quick with your little legs."

Razzy narrowed her eyes and looked up into my face.

"I can hack it."

I couldn't help but smile at the look of determination on her face.

"I guess I could bring your new carrier, and if you get tired, you could jump in. Tell you what, we'll try it on our own before hiking with Ben, ok?"

"Promise?"

"I promise."

She gave my hand a quick swipe with her raspy tongue before turning around twice in my lap and getting comfortable. I watched the evening news and zoned out to a re-run of a medical show before my eyes felt heavy.

* * *

THE NEXT THING I KNEW, someone was pounding on my front door. I woke up suddenly, my heart racing, and I felt Razzy jump off my lap. The racket continued, and I debated what I should do. I looked at my watch and saw it was just before four in the morning. Who on earth would pound at my door this early?

"Are you going to answer that?" Razzy asked softly. "I don't like the smell of whoever is out there."

Her nose was coming in handy. I trusted she knew better than I did and pulled her close.

"Shhh, let's see what they do."

I sat breathless as I listened, trying to figure out who was here. Few people knew where I lived. From the sound of it, whoever it was wasn't thrilled. The knocking continued for another few minutes before I heard my next-door neighbor shout out onto the landing.

"Knock it off! We're trying to sleep."

It sounded like whoever was at my door kicked it before swearing and stomping off. From the sound of the voice I'd guess it was a man, but I didn't know for sure. My heart rate finally slowed down, and I took a deep breath. Waking up suddenly always threw me for a loop and made me feel shaky and off-balance. Razzy jumped down off the couch, fur fluffed up, so she looked twice as big. She stalked towards the door, sniffing underneath it. I joined her and peeked out my blinds, but I didn't see any cars I didn't recognize.

"Well, Razzy, that was weird."

"I don't like it," she said, with a yawn and a stretch. "Yes, I know, big stretch, big yawn, yadda yadda yadda."

I laughed out loud. She'd beaten me to the punch with my saying.

"On that note, do you think we should try to get some more sleep? I don't need to be up for another three hours."

"I'm a cat. I never turn down a chance to sleep."

Razzy stalked back towards the bedroom, tail swishing back and forth like a question mark. I followed behind, trying to quiet my mind. It helped that my trip to the gym and the long day made me exhausted. I turned off my phone, snuggled into bed, and within a few minutes, I was out cold.

CHAPTER 12

Thursday, June 25th

$\mathcal{M}$y arm muscles woke me up before my alarm, shrieking in agony. I rolled over to grab my phone off the bedside table and whimpered at the movement. I should've known that trip to the gym wouldn't treat me well. I turned on my phone and saw I had fifteen missed calls, two voicemails, and four texts. Oh boy.

I listened to my voicemails first. They were both from Tom, and I winced as I heard him barking into my ear. He didn't say what was wrong, but I was supposed to call him back immediately. I couldn't help but gulp. I went to my texts and saw one was from Tom, two were from Ashley, and the other was from a number I didn't recognize.

It must be pretty serious for Tom to text. The office joke was he was just like the main character in the movie, Machete - he didn't text. It was in all caps and repeated what his voicemail said.

Ashley's texts let me know Tom was trying to get a hold of me, but the one from the unknown number made me pause.

I told you to leave this alone. Now you're going to pay.

I gulped and took a screenshot before looking at the details. All I could see was it was sent from a local number about an hour ago. The way it was worded sounded just like the note that was left in my car. I forwarded the text to Ben's number.

I googled the number, and it didn't come up with anything. I was striking out here. I looked across the bed and saw Razzy sleeping flat on her back, all four feet in the air. Oh, to be a cat.

"Hey, Razzy. Wake up."

Razzy went from prone to on her feet with her tail puffed out in the blink of an eye.

"Who? Is someone here again? I'll shred them!"

"Whoa, tiger. I just wanted to see what you thought of all of this."

While I cared what she thought, I was just stalling before calling Tom. Obviously, something was up, and from his tone, it wasn't good. If I was going to lose my job, a few minutes more wouldn't matter, right?

I read through the texts and summed up Tom's voicemails for Razzy. She listened while lashing her tail back and forth.

"Whoever is threatening you had better watch themselves and not come around here. I don't like it when people go after my mother," she said, flicking her claws open and shut.

"Relax, I'm sure it's harmless. My story went live and we got a reaction. That's what we wanted. Now, I guess I'll bite the bullet and call Tom."

My call went straight to his voicemail. Score! I left a message letting him know I'd be in within an hour. By the time I got back from showering, I had a new text from Ben. He promised to look into the number that sent the text, but it didn't look promising. He said it was probably from a burner phone. I smiled as I read his second text, which told me to be careful and asked me to call him if I heard anything else.

I pulled on a comfy tee and a pair of skinny jeans. Hopefully, I wasn't on my way to getting fired. I put my still wet hair up into a ponytail and headed to the kitchen to brew up some coffee. After checking to make sure Razzy's box was clean, and she had plenty of food and water, I poured half of the pot of coffee in my travel mug and called for Razzy.

"Razzy, I've got to go to work. I don't think I should bring you today."

"I'm right here. You don't need to shout. Geez."

I looked down, startled, and sure enough, she was sitting at my feet. I swear she was a ninja cat.

"Sorry, but yeah, I'll be back later. I wish you could text. We could talk during the day."

"Too hard with these," Razzy said, holding up a paw. "It's all I can do to open your reading app. But I guess I could practice."

She had a sparkle in her eye as she marched towards the couch and the iPad. Oh dear, what can of worms had I opened up now?

I trotted out, securing both locks on my door before heading down to my car. With everything going on this morning, I'd all but forgotten about the person at my door last night. I changed directions and walked up to my neighbor's door. They weren't around very often, but with any luck, they were still at home.

I rang their doorbell and waited. The door flung open, and my neighbor was standing there in an open robe and tighty-whities. It was not a good look.

"Whaddya want?"

"Hi, I'm Hannah. I live next door. I was just wondering if you got a glimpse of the person who was pounding at my door last night."

"You mean this morning at 4? I couldn't get back to sleep," he whined, scratching the hair on his protruding belly.

Ick.

"I'm sorry, it wasn't anyone I know, and it was probably someone who had the wrong address."

"Well, I didn't see them. It was too dark. Make sure it doesn't happen again," he said, slamming the door shut.

I shrugged and headed back down the stairs to my parking lot.

Burning my lip on my coffee, I winced as I pulled open the door of my Blazer and climbed in. Traffic was still pretty light, so I made it to the newsroom in record time. Great, the one day when I wanted to put off getting to work it was smooth sailing.

Waving to Ashley as I walked past, I headed straight for Tom's office. May as well get this over with, right? I pulled up short from knocking on Tom's door when I saw who was in Tom's office through the window. It was Gerald Harms. Just great. This day kept getting better and better. I bit my lip and knocked lightly.

"Enter."

I walked in with a big smile, ready to see what was going on. Tom would have my back. At least I hoped he would. I sat down next to Harms and tried to act confident.

"Hiya, Tom. Sorry I missed your call."

"Calls. Plural. As in many."

"Right, sorry I missed your calls. Hi, Mr. Harms, it's nice to see you this morning."

"Don't you give me that, you little..."

"Hey! Don't talk to my reporter like that," Tom said. "She worked hard and dug up some information. Judging from your reaction, you're not too happy with what she found. Did it get a little too close to the truth?"

"I'll be talking to the owner of this paper today. I want this girl fired! You can't have a reporter on staff who just makes things up!"

"Tell that to the Times," Tom said, leaning back in his chair.

It creaked dangerously. He spent so much time kicked back in that chair. I was certain one of these days it was going to snap and send him tumbling to the floor.

"I mean it, I will not stand for this! Our bank is a respected institution, and we will not have our name thrown around and associated with lies."

"Are they lies, Mr. Harms?" I asked, breaking into his tirade. "From where I'm sitting, you seem pretty worked up if there's nothing to the story."

His face colored bright red, and I swear I could see steam leaking out of his ears. I debated pushing him further to see what he'd say when Tom spoke up.

"Mr. Harms, I've made a note of your objection, and we'll investigate this on our end. If you feel you have to complain to the owner, go right ahead. We back our reporters. If Hannah published that story, she did it because she had hard evidence the claims are true."

"When I find out who leaked that information to you, you're both going to pay," Harms said, spitting his words.

Got him!

"So, you're acknowledging this information exists? Is that right, Mr. Harms? Would you care to comment on the evidence which shows you were involved in embezzling from First Legacy's clients?" I asked, watching for his reaction.

Harms' face went through a myriad of emotions before settling on rage. He grabbed both arms of his chair and levered himself upward. For a second I thought he would lunge at me, but he got himself under control. He stiffly walked to the door and turned around to face us.

"You'll be hearing from my attorneys. This is an internal matter and shouldn't be bandied around by the press."

He wrenched open the door and slammed it with a bang. I heard Tom chuckling and whipped my head around.

"You're laughing? That guy was nuts! He's probably gonna want me fired. I haven't been here that long. I can't lose my job!"

"Relax, Hannah. You're not going anywhere. I knew when I read your story you had proof. Hopefully, you've got it in a safe place. We've got your back, don't worry about it. Harms isn't that powerful. He just likes to act like he is. Now, tell me more about what you found."

I sat back, relieved I wasn't losing my job just yet and filled Tom in on the files from Georgia. I didn't mention her name, and I knew Tom wouldn't ask. He trusted me, and that made me feel good. He nodded as I went through everything.

"So, now I think we have a new avenue to chase. Maybe one client discovered the embezzlement and took the law into their own hands. I'll see what Ben finds out."

"You like this detective, don't you?"

"Oh, um, yeah, he seems nice. He's willing to work with us, which is nice, considering what the Times said about him."

Tom narrowed his eyes.

"I'll let it go for now, but I know you better than you think. Well, now you know why I called you so many times. Why on earth did you turn off your phone after dropping a story that hot?"

"I'm sorry, I had someone come to my apartment at four and wake me up, pounding on my door. I just wanted to get some extra sleep. I should've known better."

"All right, well, don't do it again. I'm going to trust you're going to stay on this angle and find where it leads?"

"You know it! I'll let you know as soon as I hear anything."

"Sounds good. Get to work."

And with that, I was dismissed. I walked out of Tom's office and headed for my cubicle, ready to track down information on Mark's clients. If I started with the highest dollar amounts stolen, I was sure I'd be able to narrow down who was most likely to want Mark dead.

I saw Vinnie coming down the hall and looked both ways, hoping to find somewhere to hide. Luckily, I was right by the women's restrooms. Not even Vinnie would dare to go in there. I hoped, anyway.

After ducking in there, I leaned against the counter. What a morning. At least the chaos had taken my mind off my sore arms. I moved my shoulders around, testing them. Yep, they still hurt. I walked to the door to see if the coast was clear. I didn't see Vinnie, so I headed to my cubicle and ducked in.

Once I was at my desk, I texted Ashley, setting up a lunch date away from the newsroom to talk. I opened up my laptop and paged through the file Georgia gave me. Unfortunately, everything was printed out, making it more challenging to sort through. I quickly got lost in columns of numbers and blacked out the background noise above me.

"Heard you almost got fired today. What a shame."

"Ack! Don't you ever knock?" I asked, thoroughly angry at being interrupted by Vinnie of all people.

"We're all in cubicles. We don't have doors. I can't knock on a cubicle."

"You can make your presence known somehow, can't you?"

"Whatever. Anyway, you almost got canned, huh? It sounds like you're in over your head," Vinnie said, as he craned his neck around, trying to see what I was working on.

I slammed the lid of my laptop closed and shut the folder. Taking a deep breath, I reminded myself that getting into a fight with one of my co-workers would only serve as a distraction from the biggest story in my life. I tried hard to keep it together.

"I'm not in over my head. Sometimes, when you write the truth, it makes bad people angry. I guess you wouldn't know much about that since you rarely write anything worth getting noticed."

Whoops, there went my resolution not to get into a fight with Vinnie. Insults rolled off his back like water, but if you brought his work into it, he'd be ready to go in no time flat. I bit my lip as I watched his face turn red.

"I've been working on important stories for years, whereas you waltz in here and after two short years, you've got the biggest story this paper's seen in almost a decade. How did you do it? Give Tom a little on the side?"

That did it! Any good feelings about keeping the peace and taking the high road fled faster than one of Vinnie's dates once they met his mother.

"That is a despicable thing to say. I work hard and I'm good at writing. If you don't like it, maybe you need to work on improving your own craft instead of lobbing baseless accusations at me," I said, standing up.

This was one of those times when I wished I was just a smidgen taller. It's tough to intimidate people when you're only a few hairs over five feet tall. I stood as tall as I could and squared my shoulders. I didn't have to put up with this. I gathered my laptop and files and stuffed everything in my bag.

Vinnie seemed shaken by my anger and looked like he knew he stepped over the line but still wanted to save face.

"Well, I still say it's not fair. Stories should go to the reporters who've been waiting for the longest, not little upstarts like you."

"Whatever, Vinnie," I said as I walked past, not caring I bumped him with my elbow. "I've got to work, and obviously, that's something you don't understand."

I walked past Ashley's cubicle and nodded towards the front. She knew me well enough not to ask questions. She grabbed her purse and joined me.

Ashley moved quickly to catch up with me.

"Geez, for a tiny thing, you can cover some ground when you want to. Slow down!"

I waited until we were outside to vent. Unfortunately, my venting style included angry crying, which made me angrier, resulting in more crying.

Ashley took me over to the bench by the entryway and sat me down, handing me a tissue.

"It's just not fair. I've worked so hard for this story, and to have Vinnie say I slept my way to get it just makes me so..."

The rest of my sentence got garbled up with tears. Ashley passed me another tissue, and I blew my nose, not caring that I sounded like a startled goose.

"It sucks, babe. You know how it is in this industry. That's why I'm happy with my lifestyle section. The only drama there is from brides who want their wedding coverage just so. The dudes in the office don't even read that section, let alone care about it."

"But I want hard news," I said, hiccupping.

"I know you do, and you're good at it. You just have to realize that wounded male pride comes with the territory. You gotta grow some thicker skin, girl."

I took a deep breath, willing myself to stop crying. After another swipe at my eyes, I wadded up my tissue and tossed it in the nearby bin.

"I know. It just sucks. I know it's early, but do you wanna grab lunch?"

"Let's do it," Ashley said, grabbing my arm.

"Tacos?"

"Can you ever go wrong with them?"

CHAPTER 13

*A*s we waited for our food at Ashley's favorite taco place, I inhaled half a basket of tortilla chips. I let her know what my source had said about the embezzlement angle and my overall thoughts on the case so far. Our server slid our hot plates in front of us, and I was buried in a taco when Ashley asked what I'd been dreading.

"So, how's it going with the whole talking to your cat thing?"

I choked and used the time to wipe my face and clear my throat to figure out what I wanted to say. I'd known Ashley for years and trusted her with my life, but this? This was something different. I folded my napkin carefully before risking a look up at her.

Her eyes were twinkling, and I didn't see any judgment in her expression. I took a deep breath and plunged in.

"It's cool. I always knew Razzy was the sweetest thing, but now that I can talk to her, it's hard to describe just how awesome a cat she is."

"What does she talk about? Cat things like food and naps?"

"Well, there's a little of that, but she's got some interesting insights into people."

I dove back into my taco while Ashley returned to her

chimichanga. She may prefer to write for the lifestyle section, but I knew she had a keen mind and a hard nose for finding a story. I wanted to see what else she'd ask.

"Do you think you can talk to other animals? Are you the next Dr. Doolittle?"

That made me laugh. I was a fan of both the original film and the newer one and imagined myself talking to every animal I could find.

"No, so far it's just Razzy. I tried a dog the other day, but that didn't work. I guess I don't even know if I can talk to other cats or if it's just her. Your friend Anastasia said I had something important to accomplish, but so far, I'm not sure what that is."

"If Anastasia said it, it's true. She doesn't pull any punches. I'm glad you talked to her. Who knows, maybe you'll be the next great pet detective."

"All righty then."

We shared a laugh as we finished up our meals. I took a long sip of my drink and nearly choked again when I heard a familiar voice over my head.

"Hannah, it's nice to see you again. We keep bumping into each other," Ben said, smiling. His eyes crinkled up in the corners, and a small dimple on his left cheek flashed at me.

"Oh, hi, Ben. I'd almost think you still thought I was a suspect, the way you keep popping up. Ashley, this is Ben Walsh, the detective I've been telling you about."

"Hi, Ben, I'm Ashley Wilson. Hannah's told me all about you, but I see she left out how gorgeous you are," Ashley said, extending her hand.

It's a good thing I didn't have a mirror, or I would have been able to see the bright red flush spreading across my face instead of just feeling it.

Ben laughed and turned slightly pink.

"I don't know about that, but thanks. Hannah, I couldn't find anything on the threatening text you got earlier. It's most likely a burner phone."

"Threatening text?" Ashley asked, giving me a look.

"Yeah, I might've forgotten to mention it. It wasn't a big deal, just a text telling me to stop looking into this story," I said.

"That's nuts! Hannah, are you going to be ok? I don't like the thought of you being all alone in your apartment."

"I'll be ok. I'm sure it's just a random thing. Ben, are you meeting someone? We already ate, but you can sit with us."

"Thanks," Ben said, sliding into the booth next to me. "I was thinking about that. Do you have a security system?"

It was distracting having him sit so close to me. His clean sandalwood scent wafted over. I tried to focus on what he was asking.

"I don't, but I guess I could put one in. I'll check my lease agreement."

"Let me know if you need help with it," Ben said, turning his head so he could look into my eyes.

Ashley cracked a big smile, and I glanced over at her to beg her, silently, not to tease me. She shook her head slightly but continued to grin.

"So, Ben, Hannah said you're new in town," Ashley said.

"I am. Hannah and I are planning on hiking on Saturday. I'm looking forward to checking out the trails with her."

Ashley's raised eyebrow promised me she'd be dealing out retribution towards me for burying the lede, and I knew once Ben left, there was going to be hell to pay.

"That's great. Hannah's quite the hiker, so make sure you bring your energy," Ashley said.

Our server came back with the bill, and Ben stood up to leave.

"I'd better go grab a table. A few detectives from the station are meeting me here. It was nice to see you, Hannah. Let me know about the security system. I'll call before Saturday so we can set up where to meet for our hike. Nice meeting you, Ashley."

He gave me one more smile before heading over to his table. Ashley opened her mouth, and I raised a finger, letting her know this wasn't the place for what she had in mind. She snapped her mouth shut and quirked her lips. I was really in for it.

We paid for our lunches and walked out into the bright sunshine. I lifted my face, savoring the warmth of the sun on my skin. Despite the crazy start to this day, it was turning out pretty good.

Once we were in Ashley's car and on our way back to work, she turned off the radio and smiled at me.

"So, hiking, huh? When were you going to tell me you were dating the hot detective? I was asking questions about your cat, and I could've been grilling you on your love life, you sly thing."

"Ash, quit it! We're not dating. He just mentioned he enjoyed hiking when we were having dinner and then..."

"You had dinner with him?" Ashley asked, interrupting me. "What else are you hiding under that shy exterior?"

"It wasn't a date. We were talking about the case."

"Mark my words, Hannah. He likes you. A lot. I know these things. When a man looks at you like that, he's interested."

I couldn't help but feel a little thrill, but I was desperate to keep my cool. I needed to focus on my story and worry about my non-existent love life later. I wasn't used to being in this position. Typically, we joked about Ashley's prolific love life and my utter lack of one, and I didn't know quite what to say. I loved her, but thankfully we both needed to get back to work before I ran out of ways to downplay my attraction to Ben.

Gathering my thoughts, I sat down at my desk and spread out the sheets Georgia had given me. There had to be something here. I lost myself in my work and barely noticed the newsroom emptying. After several hours, I'd highlighted many things, but I hadn't found the common thread yet.

My eyes were crossing and my head hurt, so I packed everything up and headed home. Maybe after dinner I'd give it another look. I couldn't help but feel I was missing something - and that something was big.

Razzy was waiting at the door for me, full of excitement. She shifted from foot to foot as her words garbled together with her purrs.

"Oh my goodness, I'm so happy to see you. I can't wait to show you what I learned today," she said, as she wound through my ankles.

"I'm happy to see you too," I said as I hopped my way over to the table so I could put everything down. "Did anyone come to the door today while I was gone?"

"No, it was quiet. But listen! I think I've got something figured out so we can communicate during the day when I'm not with you. Although, I would appreciate going out in the carrier again."

"Ok, let's get something to eat and you can tell me all about it."

I went to my fridge, and sure enough, it was pretty bare. A quick check of the cupboards failed to turn up even a stray can of soup. I needed to go grocery shopping. Settling for delivery food, I paged through my app, looking for something that sounded good. Razzy sat on the table and looked over my phone as I paged through the offerings.

"Ooo, let's have chicken," Razzy said, swiping her tongue around her muzzle.

"Sounds good to me. I'll get it coming."

I got everything ordered up while Razzy raced over to the couch and started pawing at the tablet.

"Ok, so I was experimenting with your messages app and figured out how to make the keyboard bigger. If I squish my paw tight, I can sort of tap out what I want to say. Here, let me show you."

My phone dinged with a text, and I glanced down at the screen. Sure enough, she'd figured out how to text. While her spelling was a little off, I couldn't help but smile at the message she'd sent.

"I love you too, Razzy. This is amazing. If it wouldn't uncover our secret, I'd take you on the road and show you off to everyone!"

"No thanks, I like our life just the way it is. I'll work on my technique, so I don't misspell everything. Tell me about your day."

She sat down on the couch and licked the fur of her ruff, adjusting it just so. I laughed, walking over to sit next to her as I filled her in on everything that happened. By the time I got to the part about the spreadsheets, the doorbell had rung with our food delivery.

I set aside a tiny piece of chicken for Razzy as I dished everything up. It didn't take me long to scarf down my dinner and clean up. Razzy jumped on the table and started pawing at my file folder. I opened it for her, spread the papers out, and sat down, curious to see what she thought. She made little purring sounds as she read, and I couldn't resist petting her little head.

"Look at this. This name keeps coming up more than the others," Razzy said, patting a line on one sheet.

I grabbed the paper and read through it, trying to see what she meant. After a few seconds, it came to me. While most of the transactions were small and occurred on random dates, these were much larger and appeared every two weeks.

"I think you're on to something, Razzy. Let me pull up this company and see what we can find."

I flipped open my laptop and typed in the name Appaloosa Enterprises into the search bar. Interesting. Other than a few generic listings, nothing was coming up. No website, no background, and no news stories. I sat back and thought for a few minutes as Razzy kept going over the files.

"Oh! I see the name again in this second section," she said, grabbing the piece of paper by the corner.

I was glad Georgia had made copies for me since this sheet now had tiny holes from Razzy's fangs in it. I took the sheet and noticed it was marked as being from Harms' account instead of Mark's. The same amount was being transferred into his account on identical dates. I thought I finally had something.

"You're a genius, Razzy! I knew I was missing something. Leave it to you to find the clue we needed! Now, I just need to figure out who runs this company and how involved they were with Harms and Mark."

I picked Razzy up and danced around with her, giving her a loud smacking kiss on the top of her head.

"Ew, I think you got chicken grease on my head," Razzy said, shooting me a glare.

"Sorry!"

I put her back on the table, and she shook a paw in disgust.

"That's going to take forever to clean off."

She jumped off the table and stalked over to the couch, settling on the cushion for what I assumed was going to be a long bathing session.

I smiled as I gathered my sheets up, ready to go back through and make a list of all the transactions that matched the company. With any luck, Razzy had blown the case wide open. There had to be a reason nothing came up under that company name. My guess was it was a shell company, operating out of another state.

I cracked my knuckles and settled down in my seat to do some serious digging online. The answer had to be out there.

CHAPTER 14

Friday, June 26th

I walked into the newsroom early the next morning, running on three hours of sleep and a full pot of coffee. My late-night search had uncovered nothing, and I needed the help of one of my sources in the state government. I shifted Razzy's bag to my other hand as I made my way to my cubicle to get started for the day.

As I put her bag under my desk and freed my laptop, I glanced around to see if anyone was in the vicinity. Satisfied I was alone, I leaned down to check on her.

"Razzy, everything ok? Sorry for jostling you around in there. I'm not quite used to carrying you around yet."

She sniffed loudly and turned around, getting comfortable.

"I'm not a sack of potatoes, you know. Maybe you can practice in your spare time."

"And I have so much of that. Seriously though, I'll try to be more gentle."

She wrapped her tail over her eyes, effectively ending our conversation. I sat back up and cracked open my laptop, ready to find out who owned Appaloosa Enterprises. Paging through my contacts, I located Fiona Washburn, my contact at the secretary of state's office. As I hit the button to place my call, I crossed my fingers. She'd always been willing to help me in the past, and I was hoping she'd come through again.

"This is Fiona."

"Hi Fiona, it's your old friend Hannah at the Post. How's it going?"

"What do you need me to look up now?"

"Hey, I call you for more than that, don't I? Sometimes it's nice just to chat."

She snorted loudly through the phone and cackled. This was a game we always played when I called.

"It's good to hear from you, Hannah. What's up in Golden Hills?"

"Same old, same old. Working on a story for a murder investigation."

"Look at you moving up through the ranks. So, what can I do to help?"

"Well, I'm not sure you're going to like this one," I said, biting my lip even though she couldn't see me. This was a big ask.

"Uh oh. Lay it on me."

"Well, I need to know if you can help me find the contact information for a shell company. I believe they're from out of state."

"What? Do you know how much hot water I'd be in if it got out I handed that information out to a reporter?"

"I know, I know. But this could be big, like figuring out who killed a man, big, Fiona. You don't have to help, but I'd appreciate it."

I said a silent prayer as I waited for her response.

"Fine, I'll do it. But you're gonna owe me big time for this one?"

"I'll double the usual order and get it sent out today."

There was a bakery here in town that made the most divine Brazilian confections, and Fiona was addicted to them. I'd sent her one a few years ago after she helped with a story, and it had become our thing.

"The things I'll do for a brigadeiro, I tell you. All right, I'll probably regret this, but lay it on me."

I gave her the name of the company and everything I knew so far. As I listened to her type in the background, I leaned back down and jostled Razzy so she could see me give her the thumb's up. She cracked an eye open and nodded her head slightly before going back to sleep.

"Any luck, Fiona?"

"I've got the contact information here. I'll text it to you. Just keep it quiet, ok? And maybe triple the order?"

I couldn't help but laugh. Fiona sure knew hard to drive a hard bargain.

"You got it and thank you! You're a lifesaver."

"Yeah, yeah. See you later, honey."

I ended the call and waited for the text to come in. A loud sneeze behind me startled me, and I turned around to see Vinnie darkening my cubicle entrance.

"Hey, Vinnie, what's up?" I asked.

I was trying to be as friendly as possible, given what had happened the day before. I wanted to put it behind me and keep from tearing his head from his neck.

"A-a-a-chooooo!"

I could feel Razzy stirring at my feet.

"Vinnie, are you ok?"

"I'm fine, fit as a fiddle, and raring to go. As usual, I might add," Vinnie said, wiping his nose with his sleeve.

I couldn't help but wince at the state of his sleeve as he pulled it away. Eww.

"Did you need something?"

"No, just wanted to see if you needed any help with your story."

Vinnie wiped at his eyes as they started running right along with his nose.

"I'm fine, but thanks. Are you allergic to something?"

"Just cats, but there aren't any cats in here, so I don't know what's triggering it. Maybe I'm developing new allergies. They say that can happen."

Oh. That explained everything. I pushed Razzy's bag further out of sight with my foot. Whoops.

"Yeah, you never know. Maybe you should go to the doctor."

"Thanks, I'll do that."

He wandered off, sneezing loudly. Grateful I'd been spared another Vinnie diatribe, I glanced back at my phone. While I'd been talking, Fiona's text came in. It included the name of a company and their phone number. As I suspected, they were out of California. I opened a new tab in my browser and typed in the name, The Sand Creek Foundation.

Their website was one of the first results, and I paged through it quickly. They were a non-profit organization specializing in rescuing horses. That made the embezzlement even worse in my book. I was about to click off their website when I noticed they had their board of directors listed. Right there in the middle of the list was a name I recognized, Georgia North.

"Would you believe that..." I said out loud as I clicked on her link.

It pulled up the site for First Legacy Bank, but the branch listed was out of San Diego, not the one here in town. I glanced around again and bent down under my desk.

"Razzy, you'll never believe it! You were right about Georgia. She was hiding something."

"When am I not right? Can I go back to sleep now?"

"Yeah, sorry, I just had to tell you."

I got up from my desk and pushed my chair under it to hide Razzy's bag. This information was big, and I couldn't contain my excitement. I walked over to Tom's office, but he was on the phone and waved me off when he saw me at the door. As I walked back to my cubicle, I saw Ashley walking in the front door, wearing huge dark sunglasses and a scarf over her hair.

"Hey, Ash, or should I say Ms. Garbo? How's your morning?"

"Hush, girl, mama needs quiet," Ashley said as she sank into her chair, holding her head. She slid the sunglasses off and winced at the fluorescent lights. I couldn't help but notice the suitcase size bags under her eyes and her pale complexion.

"Another night with the Energizer Bunny guy?"

"And how. Be a good girl and get me a cup of coffee from the break room?"

"Oh God, Ash, you can't be that bad off. You know that stuff will melt a spoon."

"That's exactly what I need right now."

I hurried off to the break room to grab her a mug of what we affectionately referred to in the newsroom as the Creature from the Black Lagoon. Gagging a little at the smell of the burnt grounds, I brought it back to Ashley.

She downed it in two gulps and slammed the mug down on her desk. As I looked on in horror, she chuckled.

"If that doesn't cure what ails me, nothing will."

"If you need to go to the hospital later for a melted stomach, let me know."

"Will do, girly. Now, I just need to rest my eyes for a second," she said, sliding her sunglasses back on and leaning back in her chair.

I tiptoed out of her cubicle and headed back to mine, temporarily deflated I didn't have anyone to share my hot scoop with. Sitting back down in my chair, I texted Ben to let him know what I'd discovered.

A few seconds later, my phone dinged with his reply.

"Really? This could be big. Thanks for sharing."

I answered him and let him know I was going to track her down. I hit send and started chewing on my thumbnail. He'd mentioned our planned hike the day before, but I was feeling nervous. What if he wanted to back out?

"You shouldn't chew on your nails," Razzy said, her soft voice barely audible over the sound of the other reporters.

"I know, I'm nervous. I can't help it."

My phone dinged again.

"Have you picked a spot for our hike tomorrow?"

I took a deep breath, feeling like butterflies were dive-bombing my insides. I answered back that I was thinking about the Golden

Loop if he didn't mind a moderate level hike. The views alone were worth it.

"Sounds good to me. I'll meet you there at 7. Looking forward to it."

The butterflies swarmed, and I couldn't sit still. I wrote back and decided I needed to get out of the office for a little. After I slipped my laptop into Razzy's carrier, I picked it up by the top handle, trying not to jostle Razzy.

I slipped out the front, hoping no one noticed Razzy inside the bag, and headed to my car. As I walked, I called First Legacy, hoping to catch Georgia at work. The woman who answered said she wasn't in, leaving me temporarily stumped. As I sat in the driver's seat, I pulled up our company database and searched for her name. Score! I found an address for her right here in town.

"Razzy, are you ready to see what's going on with Georgia?"

"Let's go!"

I wished I could take a few dozen naps a day and awake refreshed like my cat. Merging into traffic, I headed towards Georgia's house, hoping she'd be home. Once I found her neighborhood, I drove by slowly. Sure enough, there was a car parked in front of her house. I parked across the street and looked around.

It was a pleasant neighborhood, with mid-sized homes. I got out, grabbed Razzy's bag, and headed for the front door. Loud purring rumbled from within the bag as I set it on the front porch.

"Hush, Razzy, I don't want it to be too obvious I brought you with me."

"I can't help it. I purr when I'm excited."

I rang the doorbell and waited. Nothing. I rang it again while trying to peer through the tiny window. I was too short to see through it, even on my tiptoes. As I debated my next move, the door swung open, revealing Georgia.

She was dressed in a velour lounge suit, and she looked resigned as she opened the screen door.

"I was wondering how long it was going to take you to figure it out," she said, walking away from the door.

Taking that as an invitation to enter, I followed her through the entryway into the living room. Her house was beautiful, with muted peach-colored walls and ivory furniture. Even though the pieces were lovely, the room had a feeling of transience. I noticed a lack of artwork on the walls or anything personal that could be tied back to Georgia. She motioned for me to take a seat on the sofa as she sank into an ivory chair across from it.

"Thanks for letting me in."

"There's no point in hiding from you. I'll admit, when I saw you walk up it went through my mind, but I'm guessing you're a tenacious little thing. Might as well get this over with."

"All I know so far is that you're on the board of a company that was losing money to Harms and Mark. And you used to work for First Legacy in California. Do you want to fill in the blanks?"

Georgia looked away. As I watched her, I couldn't help but wonder if she'd been the one who killed Mark. I couldn't reconcile the woman in front of me being a cold-blooded killer, but stranger things have happened.

"I've been with First Legacy for twenty years. I moved up quickly and became a commercial lender in the main San Diego branch about five years ago. I've always been active in the community, working with different charities. Sand Creek was a cause that was close to my heart. I love horses, and they do so much good work. They have a sister organization here in Colorado, and they wanted to set-up a company here to help them out."

She paused and wiped her eyes.

"Were you the one who recommended Mark to them?"

"I was. He had a good reputation as an up and comer in the main branch. He was getting noticed, and I thought he would help Sand Creek out. I never thought he'd help them out of their money. They came to me about six months ago with their suspicions. I went to the bank's head in San Diego, and we worked out a way to dig into what was happening.

"We didn't want to make a big deal out of it, but we needed to find the truth. The president there arranged for me to get transferred. I've been digging into what was going on since then. I've been reporting what I've found, but nothing is happening. I knew I shouldn't have shared what I found with you, but I'm so frustrated. The people at Sand Creek work so hard to save horses, and they can't afford to lose this much money. I had to do something."

She looked deflated as soon as she finished, as if finally telling the truth had taken a massive weight off her shoulders. I heard a sympathetic mew come from Razzy's bag and hoped Georgia hadn't heard it, too.

"Georgia, did you kill Mark?"

She laughed and picked at a nonexistent spot on the arm of her chair.

"No, I didn't. Am I glad he's gone, and the embezzlement will probably stop? Hell, yes. But I didn't kill him. I wish I could say more. I've been waiting for the main branch to transfer me back. In the meantime, I'm still building a case against Harms. I think he knows something's up. Once that story of yours ran, he's been running scared. All the internal passwords have been changed, and he won't share them with me. I've been cut out. The only thing left for me is to go back home and try to help put things with Sand Creek right."

"I appreciate your honesty. For what it's worth, while I shared the information you gave me with the police, I never gave them your name. There shouldn't be too much suspicion on you."

"Thanks for that. This whole thing has shown me the ugly side of the old boys' network. I gave them more than enough proof to have Harms and Mark fired ten times over, but nothing happens. Once I get home, I'm going to take a hard look at my options."

"Good luck, Georgia. Thanks for all of your help. I hope Sand Creek gets its money back. I'll pass along the information on their sister organization to one of my friends at the paper. Ashley would love to do a story highlighting what they do."

"That'd be great. I appreciate it."

Georgia showed me out, and I walked back to my car, deep in thought. Once I was back in, I opened the door to Razzy's bag so she could stretch out for a bit. I drove home, playing music softly in the background.

"She was telling the truth that time," Razzy said as she settled into the passenger seat.

"That's good. I feel terrible for her. Do you think she killed Mark? Was she honest about that?"

Razzy licked her paw thoughtfully before passing it behind her ear.

"She was. She's a good person. And she loves animals, so in my book, she's ok."

I shrugged, willing to take Razzy's word for it.

"So, now we know it probably wasn't a client who killed Mark, that just leaves two suspects. Harms and Wesley."

"You know what I think about Harms."

"Yes, I'll never forget the back-alley bingo comment."

I laughed, and Razzy purred in amusement as we pulled into my parking lot. I was going to need to do some digging to figure out which suspect was truly the guilty party. Maybe that would keep my mind off my impending anxiety about my hiking date that was just a few short hours away. I started chewing on my thumbnail again as I thought about it.

"Don't chew your nails," Razzy said.

I shook my head and put the Blazer in park. With any luck, I'd find what I was looking for and not be a ragged mess in the morning.

CHAPTER 15

Saturday, June 27th

*L*uckily, I had no problem meeting Ben at seven in the morning for our hike. Why? Well, my brain decided waking me up at four to go over every scenario that could happen was a good idea. I disagreed, but you try telling that to my brain. I was chock full of coffee and anxiety as I waited for Ben at the trailhead. At this rate, I could probably do this trail at a full sprint and still have enough restless energy left to do it again.

Razzy had wanted to go on this hike and wasn't speaking to me when I left. Even though I knew Ben was a cat person, I wasn't sure how he'd feel about me bringing mine on our first hike together. Thinking about it brought on more butterflies. If you were potentially building a new relationship, which I wasn't since this was a friend thing (right?), were you obligated to mention you could talk to cats?

One more thing to worry about, I guess. I glanced in my rearview mirror and saw a sleek hybrid pull into the lot. It pulled up next to me, and when I looked over, I met Ben's eyes and saw his dimples as he smiled at me. Taking a deep breath, I tried to smile back as I grabbed my sling bag and got out of my Blazer.

"Good morning," he said. "What a beautiful day!"

"It's gorgeous. Just the right temperature. I'm glad we're starting early since part of this hike can get a little hot when you're out in the open."

We were dressed alike in hiking shorts, tees, and light jackets. I checked my bag to make sure I had my water bottle and did a few stretches.

"Got everything you need?" Ben asked.

"Yep, extra water, sunscreen, and Chapstick. The essential Colorado survival pack."

We both laughed and started down the trail. My anxiety fluttered away as Ben fell in next to me on the path.

"So, tell me a little about yourself?"

"Well, I was raised in a tiny town in South Dakota," I said. "We had more bars than stoplights, which I guess isn't saying much since we only had one stoplight. My parents lived on a farm my grandparents owned."

"Did you grow up doing farm chores?"

"You know it! From haying in the summer to delivering calves in the winter, there was always something to do. How about you, Ben?"

"Well, I'm a city kid. I've got an older brother. Our parents divorced when I was in high school. He went with my dad, and I stayed with my mom."

"I'm sorry to hear that. Family struggles suck."

"Do you have any siblings?"

"Nope, I'm an only kid. My friends growing up were the critters around the farm. My graduating high school class only had five kids, but I had no close friends until I went to college and met Ashley."

"Wow, that is a small school. We had probably 500 in my class alone. It must have been cool growing up in a tight-knit community."

"In some ways, yes, and in other ways, no. If you so much as sneezed the whole town knew about it, and the rumor mill had you dying of consumption by the time dinner rolled around."

He chuckled and paused as we crested a hill. The panoramic view that opened up cleansed my soul. I took a deep breath of the crisp, pine-scented air and closed my eyes. When I opened them, I found Ben staring at me with a little smile on his face.

"You love nature, don't you?" he asked.

"I do. It's my peace when everything gets crazy. Sometimes I miss the farm, but then I go on a hike and remember why I left. It's just hard to get inspired by flat land."

"I hear you. This is such a beautiful place. It's part of what drew me to the area."

We started down the path again, falling into step with one another. Ben was taller than me by almost a foot, and I appreciated the way he matched his stride with mine so I could keep up.

"Any new suspects in the Mark Brown case?"

A look of frustration creased his face, and he scrubbed his hair with his hand.

"No, I'm running into roadblocks everywhere, it seems. It doesn't help I have ten other cases on my plate either. Tell me more about your meeting with Georgia."

I stopped and opened up my bag to grab a bottle of water as I told Ben about my impressions of Georgia. He listened and nodded thoughtfully as I went through everything she'd said to me.

"After talking with her, I think she was honest," I finished.

"I agree with you. When I ran her at the start of the investigation, nothing cropped up that would lead me to believe she'd suddenly become a killer."

"I went through all the other accounts to see if there was a client with a huge amount of money missing, but I couldn't find anyone else besides Sand Creek. I think he took advantage of the fact they're out of town and wouldn't be as careful with their book work for a subsidiary. If it hadn't been for Georgia's interest, it would likely have taken a lot longer to be noticed," I said, tripping over a rock as I looked over at Ben.

Ben steadied me, his hand gentle on my arm. I couldn't help but swallow hard as I felt the warmth of his hand. He smiled.

"Careful, there. So, out of everyone left, who do you think did it?"

"I'm going with Wesley, I think. He stood to gain the most out of Mark being gone. He got the ex-girlfriend and the accounts."

"Interesting. He's on my radar, too, particularly since he doesn't have an alibi. Jordan wasn't with him since she was at the event. She didn't even try to lie for him when I asked her. She said he was probably at work, but she didn't know," Ben said.

"I need to update my story, but I have nothing new to report beyond chasing the angle of Harms and his embezzlement. That one won't be easy."

We continued down the path, pausing every few miles to soak in the beauty. We both shared stories from our childhoods and past jobs we'd had. Before I knew it, it was after twelve and we hadn't turned back yet.

"Hannah, if you're hungry, I packed some granola bars," Ben said, rummaging through his bag.

"Awesome! That will tide me over until we get back."

I found a log off the trail and positioned it so we could both sit. After a few minutes, I tucked the wrappers into my bag and took one more swig of water.

"Ready to head back to the cars?"

"Let's do it!"

We continued reminiscing as we walked, and the miles flew by. I couldn't remember the last time I'd felt so at ease with someone. All of my anxiety washed away, and I felt I could be myself with Ben. Well, almost. I still didn't quite know how to handle the cat thing, but I could cross that bridge when I got to it. If I got to it. Right?

Once we reached the trailhead, we both stood awkwardly in front of my Blazer. Ben scrubbed at his hair again and looked down.

"Hannah, would you like to come to my place and have dinner? I can't remember the last time I've had this much fun, and I'd hate for our day to end here. It's ok if you don't want to."

"I'd love to, but I'm worried about my cat. She's been home alone all day, and she was mad at me when I left."

Ben looked at me oddly for a second.

"She's a cat. Mine's always just fine being left at home."

"I know, but Razzy was mad, and I feel terrible. Still, I appreciate you asking. I've had a great time, too."

I hung my head to hide the blush spreading across my cheeks. Here I was, after a fantastic day, turning down an invitation to dinner with a hot guy because I needed to get home to my cat. I've had better moments.

I felt Ben's finger under my chin as he lifted my face.

"You're attached to her, aren't you?"

"Yeah, I am. But I had an amazing time today. I'd like to do it again, if you want to, I mean, I don't want to presume or anything, but yeah..."

I trailed off, looking down again.

"Tell you what, bring Razzy. You can swing by your house and use that new carrier you got. Heck, my cat Gus would probably love the company. It'll be like a play date."

"Are you sure?"

He smiled, and my heart warmed at the openness in his eyes.

"I'm sure. I'll text you my address."

He opened the door for me, and I slid in, smiling like a loon. I waved as I pulled out of the trailhead and headed back to my apartment.

When I opened the door to my apartment, I saw Razzy sitting there on the couch, with her back to me. I sighed and walked over to her. Typically, she met me at the door. She must still be mad at me. I put a hand on her back, and she sniffed, still not looking at me.

"Well, I guess you're still mad," I said, sitting down next to her. "That probably means you don't want to come with me to Ben's and meet his cat, Gus."

Her head swiveled, and her eyes got big.

"What did you say?"

"We've been invited to Ben's house tonight for dinner. I didn't want to come since I wanted to get home to you, so Ben said to bring you along."

"Oh my gosh," Razzy said, her words getting jumbled up with her purrs. "I'm not ready for this. I need to bathe. Oh, I just bet my fur is a mess."

She started manically swiping her tongue over her fur. I got off the couch and walked back to the bedroom.

"I've got to get cleaned up, too. We've got a few minutes. And you always look beautiful, Razzy."

Once I was out of the shower, I stood in front of my closet, paralyzed with indecision. What should I wear to a sort-of-dinner-date? I chewed on my thumbnail as I went through the hangers. What I wouldn't give for Ashley's fashion sense or half of her clothes right about now.

"Don't chew your nails."

I looked over at the doorway and saw Razzy sitting there, looking like a queen. Her fur was all fluffed up, and her ruff looked like it'd been freshly laundered.

"You never have to worry about what to wear, you lucky cat."

She hopped up on the bed and looked at my closet.

"Go with the purple shirt. It brings out the green in your eyes. A nice pair of black skinny jeans and your flats. You don't want to trip and fall on your face. I've seen you in heels, and it never ends well. He already knows you're short, so there's no point in pretending."

"Um, thanks, I guess."

Not sure what to make of her fashion critique, I got dressed and pulled a comb through my wet hair. I turned to leave, catching sight of Razzy on the bed.

"Really? That's all you're going to do with your hair?" Razzy asked, cocking her head to the side.

"Hey, I am who I am. I don't see the point in going all out."

"Humans."

She jumped down and stalked towards the front door, arranging her fur as she sat next to her carrier.

"All right, I think that's everything. Jump on in."

"I will majestically enter the carrier, but I will not 'jump on in' as you so eloquently put it."

"La-di-dah, your highness. Hop in."

She slowly stepped in the carrier, dragging it out just to torture me. I didn't miss her wink as she settled herself in her carrier.

"Oh, try not to jostle me too much. It took forever to get my ruff arranged."

I rolled my eyes as I placed her in the back seat. Grabbing my phone, I copied Ben's address into my mapping app and started the car. He didn't live that far away, only a few miles. Even with traffic, it wouldn't take us long to get there.

My butterflies were back in full force, and they were far more organized than last time. It felt like they were performing advanced aerial maneuvers in my stomach as I walked up to Ben's door, Razzy in tow.

"Ok, Razzy. Here goes. Let's be on our best behavior tonight. No hissing, no shedding if you can help it, and no clawing anything."

The delicate snort that came from her carrier left me no doubt what she was thinking.

"As if I would do any of those things. I'm not the one who didn't bring wine or a small gift for the host. Heathen."

I rang the bell, and within a few seconds, Ben opened it. He must have just showered since his hair was still a little wet. He was wearing a pair of faded jeans and a tight-fitting black tee. Be still my heart.

"Hannah! Come on in."

Ben held the door open for me, and I walked in, placing Razzy's carrier on the floor next to the door. His apartment was nice and didn't scream bachelor. It was a far cry from the guys I'd dated in college. Instead of mismatched furniture and ripped posters, Ben had a leather couch, nice artwork, and unstained carpet.

"Thanks for inviting me over. Your place is so nice," I said. "Is it ok if I let Razzy out?"

"Of course. Gus! Come here, bud."

One of the biggest cats I'd ever seen sauntered over to the entryway. He was a beautifully marked tabby with a pair of large hazel eyes.

"Hi, Gus, it's nice to meet you," I said as I knelt to unzip Razzy's carrier.

"Nice to meet you, too," Gus said in a deep, raspy voice.

In shock, I snagged my shirt sleeve on the zipper. I struggled with it, not missing Razzy's embarrassed little mew from the carrier. Apparently, I could talk to more than just my cat. The implications raced through my head as I kept jerking on my sleeve.

"Here, let me help you," Ben said, reaching down to separate the two.

I couldn't help but blush as our hands made contact. Finally freed, I unzipped Razzy's carrier the rest of the way and opened the flap so she could step out.

If there was such a thing as a cat supermodel, Razzy could have been one. She slowly emerged, every hair in place, before sitting down politely in front of Gus. His eyes flared as they exchanged sniffs.

"You gorgeous creature, where have you been all my life?"

"Fresh! We just met. My name is Razzy. I assume you're Gus?"

They continued sniffing one another as Ben and I stood up. He laughed as the two cats meowed back and forth. I wished he could have understood the running commentary between the two, and it was all I could do to keep it together as they chatted back and forth. Ben led me to the kitchen where something delicious was simmering on the stove.

"I hope you like pasta," Ben said, walking over to the stove to stir the sauce. "I make my sauce from scratch."

"It smells amazing," I said, looking around. "Is there anything I can help with?"

Between the way he decorated his place and his cooking skills, I couldn't help but be impressed. This guy was next level.

"I've got the garlic bread in the oven already, but if you want to mix a salad, that'd be great."

He opened up the fridge and pointed everything out to me before grabbing two bowls and placing them on the counter.

We prepared everything in companionable silence as I listened to the two cats get to know one another. I didn't want to eavesdrop too much, but they were so darn cute together.

"Wait, you're saying your human understands you?" Gus asked Razzy.

"She does, every word. It wasn't always that way, but ever since she met your human, she's been able to understand me."

"It's a miracle," Gus said, turning his head and looking at me with awe.

I giggled at his expression, and Ben glanced over at me.

"What's so funny?"

"Oh, nothing, just something I heard. Earlier. Something I heard earlier," I said, staring down at the lettuce to avoid eye contact.

I needed to watch myself. He probably already thought I was a little odd since I nearly didn't come to spend time with my cat. The last thing I needed was for him to think I was entirely around the bend.

"Let me grab the dressing. I made some the other night. It should still be good," he said, walking back over to the fridge.

What kind of culinary heaven had I landed in? A hot guy who cooked, made his sauce, and his own salad dressing?

"Excuse me, miss, but before you leave, could I ask you a few things?" Gus asked, sitting politely at my feet.

"Of course," I said.

"Of course what?" Ben asked.

Shoot! I'd done it again.

"Of course, the salad dressing should still be good. I think it lasts forever, doesn't it?"

Whew, nice save, Hannah! Ben looked at me before shaking his head and pulling the dressing out of the fridge. I looked down at Gus and hoped he could understand my facial expressions. Razzy seemed to catch on and called him away into the living room.

"I'll just drain the pasta, and we can eat," Ben said, sliding the garlic bread out of the oven.

I took a big sniff of the bread and nearly swooned. If it tasted half as good as it smelled, I'd probably eat the whole loaf. We worked together to get everything plated up and carried it to his kitchen table. Razzy and Gus were lying next to one another on the couch, watching us while they whispered back and forth. They were too far away for me to catch what they were saying, which was probably a good thing.

We dug into our meal, and I couldn't help but groan aloud as the flavors danced on my tongue.

"What's in this sauce? It's the best I've ever had," I said.

"It's an old family recipe. I'm glad you like it."

"Like it? I love it," I said as I twirled more pasta onto my fork. "I've never met a man who could cook like this."

"I get a lot of ribbing in the department. I like to cook, drive a hybrid, and have a cat. I'm sure you can guess what they say. It doesn't matter, though. Let them talk. Gus is perfect for me. I'm always gone, and a dog just wouldn't work. When I adopted him I was looking for a dog, but he claimed me. Let out the biggest meow when he saw me and latched on with his claws. He wouldn't let go, and truthfully, I'm glad he didn't."

"That's so awesome. Razzy's adopted, too."

We talked about the various pets we'd had growing up as we finished our meal. I used the last of my garlic bread to swab up the sauce on my plate, not missing Razzy's horrified gasp from the couch.

Ben chuckled as I froze.

"Go ahead. I take it as a compliment you're that dedicated to finishing it."

I popped the bread in my mouth and closed my eyes as I finished it.

"Since you made such an amazing dinner, I'll clean up," I said, grabbing my plate. "It's the least I can do."

"Suits me just fine. I love cooking, but I'm not a big fan of dishes."

Ben helped me gather up all the plates and then went into the living room. I didn't miss the way he stroked Gus' head lovingly and held out his hand to Razzy. She gently bumped her head into his hand, and my heart melted a little. Gus jumped down and joined me in the kitchen.

"Sorry about earlier, but it's just so hard to believe you can understand me. Do you think you could get Ben to change up the food he gets me? It tastes terrible, and I only eat it because it's the only thing we have. I know I should be grateful. God knows I've gone without food before, but it's awful."

"I'll do my best," I said as quietly as possible.

"What was that, Hannah?"

Gosh darn it, this man has the hearing of a bat!

"I said, I'll do my best to load the dishwasher right."

Please let him buy it. I thought as I rinsed another dish.

"Oh, I don't care about that. However, you do it will be fine."

That was close. I finished up the dishes and winked at Gus as I walked back to the living room. I picked up Razzy and settled her on my lap as I sat next to Ben.

"Thanks again for an amazing supper," I said, trying to bring up Gus' request in the conversation.

"I appreciate you coming over," Ben said, smiling at me. "I don't have many people over to my place. Work is always so busy I just haven't had time to make friends. Lucky for me, I've got this guy."

He picked up Gus and ruffled his hair. Gus looked at me, pointedly.

"Um, speaking of food, what kind of food do you give Gus?"

Ben looked at me strangely.

"Oh, um, I'm not sure. Kibble of some sort. Why?"

"Just curious. There was this food I used to give Razzy, and she never liked it. She loves this new brand. I'll text you a picture of the bag when I get home."

Gus winked at me and let out a loud purr.

Ben looked down at Gus before shaking his head.

"Would you like to watch a movie?" he asked.

"Sure. I can't stay long, but that would be nice," I said, hoping he understood my subtext.

I liked the guy a lot, and he was hotter than any man had a right to be, but I wasn't ready for anything more than dinner and a movie at this point. His jade green eyes twinkled, and his dimple flashed briefly as he shot me a smile.

"I've got to work early tomorrow morning, so that's fine. Are you a fan of Marvel?"

"Heck, yes!"

"I recorded Ant-Man on my DVR and haven't watched it yet."

"That's the best movie! Let's watch it!"

We sat next to each other on his soft leather couch and enjoyed the movie. As I watched the cats snuggle close to one another, I couldn't help but be filled with happiness. Maybe this was the start of something extraordinary.

CHAPTER 16

Monday June 29th

*M*onday morning rolled around far too quickly for my liking. After slogging my way through Sunday, trying to find a new angle for my story, I finally gave up and spent the rest of the day hanging out with Razzy. She was bubbly and full of energy, still jazzed up over meeting Gus. I might have felt the same way about Ben, but I was trying to play it cool. We'd been up half the night talking, and so far, my three cups of coffee hadn't helped resuscitate my brain.

I was in a fog as I gathered up my things to head into work. Since I needed to focus, Razzy was going to stay home today. She was currently sulking on the couch, swiping her foot slowly over the tablet. I bent down to kiss her on the forehead and was rewarded with a paw being flicked in my direction. Ok then, off to work.

As I locked the door, I heard someone approach me behind me. Figuring it was a neighbor, I didn't bother to turn around and focused on getting my key into the deadbolt lock. Apparently, the caffeine hadn't improved my brain function or my motor skills. I had just gotten the key fitted in the lock when I felt someone grab my arm. My eyes flew up to the window and met Razzy's concerned blue gaze right before everything went black. My last coherent thought was for her safety.

* * *

THE NEXT SENSATION I was aware of was the feeling of an overly large and excessively saliva-laden tongue swiping over my face. Sorry if that sounds gross, but imagine how it feels. I heard odd grunting, snuffling noises that were strangely familiar. I cracked open an eye and beheld the smiling doggy face of a pug.

I knew this pug! This had to be what's his name... Pookie something. My addled brain finally came together in a snap. This was Jordan's dog. I'd been hit over the head and kidnapped in front of my apartment. I was apparently at the mercy of a smelly Instagram-famous pug and most likely her owner. Unless Pookie-kins was branching out into kidnapping, my best guess was Jordan was to blame.

"Pookie-kins, you shouldn't be by that nasty reporter. You'll probably get fleas," Jordan said from somewhere to my left.

I debated pretending I was still unconscious, but I couldn't let that insult slide.

"I think it's more likely I'll drown in his drool than give him fleas. What the actual hell? Why did you kidnap me?"

I rolled over to glare at her, wincing as a spike of pain lanced through my head. My hands were tied behind my back, so I could only shift to my side before I couldn't roll anymore.

From my limited viewing angle, I spotted Jordan leaning against a desk. This girl always seemed to lean on something but then again, if I was built like her, I might need extra support, too. Her long hair was in a ponytail, thrown over her shoulder, and she was petting it thoughtfully as she looked at me. I couldn't get the vision of a cut-rate Bond villain out of my head. I could see my bag sitting next to her on the desk, and I wished for once I'd put my phone in my pocket. Maybe I could distract her and get to my bag.

"I didn't kidnap you, silly. That would be like, really hard. I just made it happen. That's what I do. I make things happen. And you've been making that really hard."

"Sorry about that, I guess. So if you didn't bash me over the head and bring me here, who did? And where exactly is here?"

Jordan rolled her eyes and snapped her fingers for her dog. I couldn't take my eyes off those long, stiletto-shaped nails. She might not have been the one to hit me, but I sure didn't want those nails anywhere near my face. Pookie-kins reluctantly stopped snuffling around me and shuffled over to her, leaving another doggy emission in his wake. Could this day get any better?

"Like I'm going to tell you where you are. That would be totally stupid. I had a friend grab you for me and bring you here. It was genius, if I may say so. Harmie's been so uptight lately about you, and frankly, I was sick of listening to him whine about it. I got you out of the way so he can focus on better things. Like me."

"Wait, you said Harmie. Do you mean Gerald Harms?"

"Duh, who else would I mean? We had a perfect thing going until Mark mucked it all up. And then you came along with your questions and your articles. It really got to be too much, you know?"

"My apologies."

"You should be sorry! It's been so hard for Harmie lately. Thanks to your article, the main office ordered an audit or something at the bank, and he's been so upset."

"How on earth are you involved with someone like Harms? I just can't put the two of you together. I thought you were with Wesley."

She snorted and flipped her ponytail back over her shoulder.

"Wesley? As if. That was all part of the plan. We knew he was close to Mark, and I needed to see if he was a threat and knew what was going on. He's a nobody who's going nowhere. A girl like me deserves the best, you know? Why stick with a lender when you can have the president of the bank?"

"But Harms is just a branch manager. And he's married, so..."

"He's leaving that witch! He told me so. He was just getting ready to do that when your story broke and threw a wrench in his plans. It's all your fault. I was so close to getting what I wanted. Now, I have to wait. I hate waiting!"

"Sweetie, I hate to break it to you, but his type never leaves the wife. They string along their young, pretty flings until it's time to get a new one."

Jordan's eyes narrowed, and she walked over to me with her dangerously sharp heels.

"You take that back," she said as she kicked me in the side.

Ow. They may have been expensive high heels, but they felt like steel-toed boots. I needed to play this smarter. The more I could get her to talk, the better my chances were of figuring out where I was and how to get out of this mess.

"I'm sorry, I'm sure in your case, he was going to make an exception," I said, trying to cover up how much my ribs hurt.

"That's better. We had it all planned out. Once Mark was out of the way, Harmie was going to get a big promotion, and then we were going to move to California."

"How on earth did you get hooked up with Harms? I thought you were dating Mark?"

She examined her nails as she leaned back against the desk.

"I was dating Mark, at least for a little while. I'm all about upward mobility, you know? I thought he had a great shot at a future, and he kept getting promoted, but Harms has it all. The nice car, the huge house, the maids. I met him at one of the work picnics. Mark was off flirting with Harmie's wife, and we got to talking. I never thought we'd have so much in common, you know?"

I really didn't know, but I was so fascinated, I just nodded to keep her talking.

"So, who had the great idea to embezzle from the bank's clients?"

"That was me. I have to say it was one of my better ideas. I mean, there's so much beautiful money in a bank. Mark was all on board. He wanted to go big, but I convinced him to keep the amounts small, so they could pass as clerical errors. He was mean to me, though, and I didn't like him flirting so much, so I might have let it slip to Harmie what he was doing."

She giggled and pulled her ponytail back over her shoulder.

"I bet Mark didn't appreciate that."

"He never even knew! Harmie is so smart. He pulled the records and started duplicating the withdrawals. I cut Mark loose so I could focus all of my time on my Harmie."

"You said something about Mark mucking it all up. How did he find out?"

She made a face and picked up Pookie-kins, startling another emission out of the poor dog. What on earth did she feed him?

"One of his clients must have complained or something. Anyway, he came to Harms and threatened to go public. Everything we were working towards was about to come crashing down, but I took care of that."

"I thought you had an alibi for that night?" I asked, appalled at her level of calculation.

"Oh, I did, I'm not stupid. I had my friend take care of it for me."

"Some friend. I'm guessing it's the same one who gave me this knot on the head?"

"He's so helpful. He's just the best!"

"Yeah, there's nothing like a helpful hitman."

"I know, right?"

I couldn't help but snort. This girl was truly a piece of work.

"I suppose it's the same guy who bashed out my window in my car, too, huh?"

"What? No, I didn't ask for that. Unless it was a free add-on, hmmm, I should check."

"So, let me see if I've got this straight. You got Mark to embezzle, hooked up with Harms, got Mark out of the way, and put one over on poor, hapless Wesley? What else do you have planned?"

She looked like she was going to answer and then stopped, wagging a manicured finger in my direction.

"I can't tell you that, silly. It would spoil the surprise."

Oh yay, a surprise! Somehow, I guessed I didn't want to know what this surprise was. Based on her twisted logic to this point, I could only imagine what else she had dreamed up.

"What do you plan to do with me? You can't just keep me tied up here."

She put Pookie-kins back on the floor and smiled at me while cocking her head. The pug ran back over to me and gave me another swipe of his tongue over my face. Lovely.

"First, I need to know what you've told the police and what else you know. After that, I have a special plan in mind for you."

"Well, honestly, it's become apparent I was way off target with Mark's killer. I was focusing on Wesley. I'd feel bad about it but he's a tool, so there's that, I guess. As for what I know, you've helpfully filled in a lot of the blanks, so I think we're on the same page."

Maybe she'd buy it and not come at me with those talons she called fingernails. She looked at me for a long time, eyes narrowed. I couldn't help but hold my breath as I waited for her next move.

"I think you're telling the truth. I almost feel bad about what's coming next, but hey, a girl's gotta do what a girl's gotta do. You just got in my way, honey. It's nothing personal."

With that, she snapped her fingers again and stuffed Pookie-kins in her giant purse. She swung it over her shoulder, and once again, it looked like the poor pug was going to be sick.

"You can't just leave me here," I said, hoping she'd forget my bag so I could grab my phone and get help.

"Oh, I know that, silly. Duh. My friend's coming back here in a few minutes to finish this off. Like I said, no hard feelings, though."

She walked out of the room, and my heart soared. She'd left my bag! I was trying to figure out how to roll to my feet when I heard her heels tapping on the floor.

"Whoops! Almost forgot this," she said, scooping my bag up before turning to leave again.

She flipped the light switch as she left, plunging me in darkness. I heard a metal door scraping shut, and then all was quiet.

Ok, so I was trapped in a building with no idea where I was, and I didn't have a phone. Plus, the ever-so-helpful hitman was due to arrive any second. My heart raced, and my palms got sweaty. This was not good.

I took a deep breath and tried to stop panicking. First things first, see if I can get my hands free. I remembered from a television show that you had to get your arms in front of you, so I struggled to sit up. How was I going to do this? After a few contortions and a whispered promise to go to a yoga class if I ever got out of this, I worked my hands to the front of my body.

Finally! I stood up, walked over to the desk, and fumbled with the drawers, praying I'd find a letter opener or something sharp so I could cut the rope. Coming up empty, I made my way over to the wall, searching for the light switch. Success!

I was in an office that was attached to a large shop area. Maybe there'd be something in there that I could use. After a few tries, I got my tied hands around the doorknob and it turned. The lights in the shop were all off, and there weren't any windows. At first, I thought I'd search for a light switch, but common sense prevailed. Hands tied or not. I needed to get out of here. I put my hands up on the wall to guide me as I looked for the door I'd heard Jordan use. It had to be around here somewhere.

Halfway down the shop, I heard a pickup outside cut off. Oh no, this had to be Jordan's friend. I ran back into the office area, desperate to find a place to hide. I scrambled under the desk, and for once, it was a good thing I was so small. I hunched up in a ball and tried to quiet my breathing.

I could hear heavy footsteps approaching the office. My thoughts flashed to Razzy. What on earth was she going to do, locked in my apartment with no one to come for her? How long would it take my co-workers to figure out that I was missing? She could starve to death and never know what happened to me. I couldn't go down without a fight! Even with my hands tied, I needed to get out of this alive.

The footsteps sounded on the other side of the desk, and I held my breath. If only I had a weapon of some sort. I was seeing little black spots in my vision from holding my breath. What was I going to do?

Just as the footsteps rounded to the front of the desk, the metal door in the shop scraped open again. Whoever was looming over me stopped and cursed softly. Who on earth was here? This place was like Union Station!

"Hannah?"

Oh my gosh, that sounded like Ben. Either my fevered brain was imagining things, or Ben was actually here. The man standing next to the desk froze and for a second, I was worried he would crawl under it with me.

"Hannah!"

What was I going to do? If I shouted to warn Ben, I'd be lucky to live for the next few seconds. If I stayed quiet, Ben could get hurt. Concern for Ben won out, and I acted impulsively. Slowly, I snaked my foot out from under the desk and kicked the guy standing there as hard as I could.

"What the hell?"

There, at least Ben knew someone was here. I closed my eyes hard and prayed whatever happened would be quick and painless. At least with Ben here, he'd hopefully think of Razzy and make sure she was ok.

"Stop right there, put your hands up," Ben said from the doorway.

"Hey man, I'm not doing anything wrong, I'm just, uh, looking for something."

Wait just a minute. I knew that voice. It sounded super familiar.

"Keep your hands where I can see them."

From my vantage point under the desk, I could see the man was reaching for something in his waistband. Not even thinking of the danger, I got my feet under me and launched myself at his legs. I could hear Ben shouting to get down, but I wanted to make sure he wouldn't get shot. Fists balled, I kept bringing them up and down on the guy's midriff, hoping to keep him busy until Ben could get him subdued.

"Hannah, I've got this, it's ok."

It took me a second to process what Ben was saying. I looked up at the guy on the floor's face and recognized him immediately. It was Tim Waters.

"No way! I thought you were a nice guy," I said as I struggled to my feet. "You're the helpful hitman?"

Tim shrugged and held his hands up as Ben cuffed first one hand and then the other. He barked a command into his radio, and the room filled up with uniformed officers. The whole scene seemed like a blur as Tim was marched outside.

"Hannah, what were you thinking? You could have been killed!"

Ben's voice cracked, and his face had gone pale underneath his tan. He pulled me in close, and I buried my head into his chest as the adrenaline oozed out of my system. I was a shaking mess. Ben kissed me firmly on the top of my head.

"I won't say I'm sorry because I'm not," I said, swiping at my nose with my hand. "I saw him reaching, and I didn't want you to get hurt. How did you know I was here?"

Ben looked at me strangely.

"You told me where you were. I got a text from you with a pin to your location. I was worried sick when you didn't answer your texts, so I headed this way with backup as soon as I got it."

"Oh, yeah. Um, I must have forgotten about that with all the chaos."

Suddenly, clarity hit. My beautiful, precious little cat must have used the find my phone app on my tablet and sent him the directions with the messaging app. How on earth was I going to explain this?

CHAPTER 17

*M*y mind raced faster than Ben's car as he took me back to the police station. Razzy had saved the day with her quick thinking, but I didn't know how I would explain what happened to Ben. The best I could hope for was he wouldn't find out about my missing phone.

As we drove, I told Ben the essential details, and he radioed the information back to the department. With any luck, Jordan and Harms would be behind bars soon.

Within a few minutes, I was seated across from Ben's desk with a blanket wrapped around my shoulders and a hot cup of coffee cradled in my hands. Even though it wasn't cold, I just couldn't get warm. Ben was due to come back and take my statement, and I was using the time by myself to go over everything in my head. Once I was done here, I needed to get my story filed at the paper. This was going to be big!

Ben walked back into his office and put a hand on my shoulder. I leaned into his arm and closed my eyes. I was just so glad we were both ok.

"I called Ashley to come get you once you're done with your statement. I wish I could take you home myself, but..."

"You're going to be tied up here for a while. Thanks for doing that," I said, interrupting him.

He took a shuddering breath as he sat down at his desk. His face was still pale, and his light green eyes troubled as he searched my face.

"Are you sure you're ok with giving your statement now? You can wait if you need to."

"No, I'm fine. I don't want to forget anything, and it's best to do it now."

"Ok, I'm ready when you are," Ben said.

I started my story at my apartment and took my time to make sure I was relaying every detail I remembered, no matter how insignificant it seemed. After what had happened, I didn't want Jordan getting away with anything. By the time I got to the part where she had kicked me in the ribs, Ben hitched in a breath and winced as if he'd been kicked, too.

"I'm so sorry you had to go through all of this," he said, interrupting my story.

"No, it's ok," I said, putting the empty coffee mug on his desk. "It was all worth it to get someone like that off the street. She's diabolical. Have your guys picked her up yet?"

"Not yet, but we'll find her. We've got guys at the airport and on the highways. She won't get away."

"I still can't believe Tim was helping her. I thought he had an alibi for the time when Mark was killed."

"We'll be checking into it. He could have had someone lie, or he might have left and come back, and no one noticed. There's still a lot of work to be done on this case. Is there anything else you remember?"

I thought for a second before shaking my head.

"That's it for now. I've got to file my story, so I might remember something else. If I do, I'll let you know right away."

Ashley came striding into Ben's office, looking ready to wage war.

"Oh, my God, Hannah. Are you ok? I came as soon as Ben called."

She rushed over to me and hugged me hard. I wrapped my arms around her and let my blanket fall into the chair.

"Thanks for coming, Ash. It's so good to see you."

"Why didn't you answer your phone?"

"Sorry, Jordan took my bag with my phone. I sure hope I get it back," I said before realizing I'd made a mistake.

Ben snapped his head up and met my eyes. I looked away, not wanting to lie to him.

"I thought you had your phone," he said.

"No, Jordan had my bag the whole time and took it with her. When you bring her in, hopefully, I'll get it back," I said, making eye contact with him again.

I didn't miss the troubled expression that crossed his face. He opened his mouth and then seemed to think better of it, shaking his head.

"Well, if that's everything, I'll let Ashley get you home," he said, a distant tone making its way into his voice.

I could almost feel ice form in the room. My shoulders slumped. If I told him my secret, would it just make it worse?

"Ok, sounds good. I'm ready to go, Ashley."

She seemed to understand something was off and shepherded me out of the station and into her car. I was so worried about Ben's reaction, I said nothing about Ashley's insane driving. On a typical day, she'd put a Formula One racer to shame, and today was not a typical day. She was quiet during the whole trip, another anomaly, but I kept my mouth shut.

Once we were at my door, she put a hand on my arm.

"I want to hear it all, especially about why you're so upset. I didn't miss what happened between you and Ben there."

I tried to smile but missed the mark as tears started streaming down my face.

"I will, but I need to talk to someone else first," I said, opening the door.

"Mama, mama, mama, oh, I'm so glad you're ok," Razzy said, purring, meowing, and talking all at the same time.

She leaped into my arms and rubbed her head hard against my chest. Her purrs reverberated through the living room as we walked in. Ashley shut the door and seemed to understand I needed a minute with Razzy.

"You're an amazing cat. You know that, Razzy? You saved my life."

"I wasn't sure my idea would work, but it was the best I could come up with."

"How did you know what to do?"

"Well, you know I've been practicing with that messaging app. I thought about texting you, but I didn't know if you still had your phone on you or what they'd done to you. But I saw the find my phone app you have installed, and the idea hit me. You had Ben's number in your messaging app, and I figured it was my only chance to help you."

"You genius girl," I said, holding her tight.

She wrapped her little paws around my neck, and we stayed like that as Ashely rummaged around the kitchen. When she came into the living room, she was carrying two mugs.

"I didn't think you needed any more caffeine, so I found this old herbal tea bag in your cupboard," she said, taking a tentative sniff of a mug before handing it to me. "I think it's still good."

"Thanks, Ash, you're the best," I said as I untangled an arm from around Razzy and grabbed the mug.

"You want to tell me about it? I heard what you said to Razzy, but I don't know what she said to you."

Ashley sat next to me on the couch, and I told her everything. I just let it all out until I was a sobbing mess at the end.

"And I don't know what to do about Ben," I said, hitching a breath in between sobs.

Razzy nuzzled my face and licked it with her sandpapery tongue. Well, at least I wouldn't have to worry about exfoliating later. I had that going for me, at least.

Ashley was quiet as she sipped from her mug. She placed it down on the coffee table and turned to look at me.

"I think you should tell him. Tell him everything. If he's worth keeping around, he'll understand. Hannah, you're an amazing woman, and any man would be lucky to have you. If he can't handle it, you don't need him in your life."

"Oh, Ashley, I don't know if I can," I said, as a new wave of tears threatened to fall.

"You can do anything. Look at you. The little farm girl from South Dakota has sure grown up a lot from when I first met you in college. You're on your way to an amazing career as a reporter. You've got more drive than most people I know, and you've been given an amazing gift to talk to your cat. If he can't handle that, who needs him?"

"I hope you're right, Ash."

"I always am," she said, as she hugged me, squishing Razzy between us. "I'd better get back to work. Are you going to be ok?"

"Yep, I'm good. Thanks for listening. I've gotta file my story," I said, standing up and putting Razzy on the couch.

Ashley followed me to the door, laughing as we walked.

"You're the best reporter I know," she said before heading out.

I smiled and sat down at the table before realizing my laptop had been in my bag.

"Son of a biscuit!"

"Mama, what's wrong?"

"I lost my laptop and my phone, and I need to get this story in. I'll use the tablet."

I grabbed it off the coffee table and got to work, feverishly typing in my account of the story. I read through it again, unable to believe all that happened so far this day. Satisfied I had a winning story on my hands, I hit submit and entered the story into the paper's portal.

Realizing I was starving, I went into the kitchen, hoping against hope that food had materialized while I was gone. I really needed to go to the grocery store.

"Razzy, how do you feel about jammies, pizza, and a movie?" I asked, heading back into my bedroom.

"Sounds like the perfect night at home."

I got into my fuzzy pajama pants and tossed on a tank top before using the tablet to place an order with my favorite pizza place. Paging through my DVR, I looked for a movie to zone out to.

"Wonder Woman ok with you, Razzy?"

She jumped up on the couch and placed a soft paw on my leg.

"You're my superhero, but sure, we can watch that."

"Hey, you're my hero! I don't know what would have happened to me if you hadn't thought to send my location to Ben."

She chirped softly, and I grabbed her into another hug. Who would have thought finding a dead guy and learning I could talk to my cat would end up changing my life so much?

The doorbell sounded, jolting me back to awareness. I looked through the peephole and confirmed it was the pizza guy before opening the door. I'd had enough surprises for one day. I was working on my second piece when the doorbell sounded again.

"Coming," I mumbled as I grabbed a napkin to wipe the grease off my mouth on the way to the door.

A quick peek revealed Ben standing on the other side of the door. My heart started racing, and I wiped my palms on my fuzzy pants. Which reminded me I was standing there in my jammies. Oh well, I thought, as I opened the door. What's the worst thing that could happen?

Ben looked solemn as I opened the door. I noticed he had my bag in his hand.

"You caught Jordan?" I asked, motioning for him to come in.

"We did. I got your stuff and made sure your phone was in there. I figured you'd need your laptop for your work, so I swung by."

"Do you want to sit down?

"Um, sure, I guess."

Well, that didn't sound good. I took a deep breath, ready to face the music. Ashley was right. If I wanted to get serious with this guy, I couldn't keep secrets from him. I needed to come clean.

Razzy purred as he sat next to her on the couch, and he absent-mindedly stroked her head as I joined them.

"So, I'm guessing you have some questions?" I asked, ready to rip the proverbial band-aid off in hopes it would hurt less.

"I think you know I do," he said, looking into my eyes. "How did you send me your location if you didn't have your phone?"

"Well, it's a long story," I said.

And I told him. Everything. From the moment I discovered I could understand Razzy to her sending him the text that saved my life. Once I was done, I closed my eyes, unwilling to see his reaction. I wasn't sure I could handle it.

He started laughing. Hard. Excuse me? That was not the reaction I thought he would have.

"That's a good one. You should be a novelist instead of a reporter," he said, wiping his eyes. "Now tell me what really happened. Your neighbor saw you were taken and used your tablet to send me the information? Something, anything, rather than it was your cat."

"No, it was Razzy. Here, I'll show you."

I grabbed the tablet and showed him the messaging app as I looked at Razzy, begging her silently to help me out.

He read the text and handed the tablet back to me.

"That proves nothing. Like I said, maybe it was your neighbor. You said you didn't get the door locked, so they might have done that."

"Why wouldn't they just use their phone to call the police? How would they know to text you? And have you ever met my neighbor? Ugh."

Ben looked like his mind was about to crack. I needed to say something, make him see I was telling the truth.

"You know how I asked you to switch Gus' food? He asked me to tell you. He hates the food you give him."

I put the tablet in front of Razzy and opened the messaging app. She looked at me and nodded.

"Not enough to convince me, it's too easy."

Razzy chirped to get my attention, pausing in her efforts with the messaging app. I leaned down to her as she whispered in my ear. I blushed as I realized what she was saying.

"Gus says you sleep in the nude," I said, turning even redder as I met his eyes.

That was definitely interesting information to file away for later, but I wasn't sure how much help it would be right now.

Ben blushed and looked away. Apparently, Gus was right. His phone dinged, and he slid it out of his pocket. Razzy looked at me triumphantly and gave me a nod.

Ben's hand started shaking as he read the text and passed me his phone. The message read:

Hi, this is Razzy

He stood up abruptly, sending the tablet tumbling to the floor. He looked wild-eyed and even more pale than before.

"I don't know what's going on here, but you're freaking me out," he said, grabbing his phone from me as he backed towards the door.

"I'm sorry, Ben, I'm not trying to freak you out. But I needed to tell you the truth."

"And this is the truth? I'm sorry, Hannah. I really like you, but I think you need help. This is insane," he said before walking out the door.

I shut the door behind him and leaned against it. Tears started running unchecked down my face. Razzy jumped down from the couch and wound her way around my legs.

"I'm sorry, Mama. I did my best," she said, her eyes rounding.

"I know you did, sweetheart."

I picked her up and held her close as I switched off the television and headed to bed.

CHAPTER 18

Thursday, July 2nd

*A*s I sat in the third row in the press room at the police station, I marveled over everything that had happened in the past twelve days. Once my story had gone public, the next few days were a complete blur. Tom, my editor, was thrilled with my piece, while Vinnie was still mad I'd gotten the story, let alone been the one to break the case wide open.

I chewed on my thumbnail as I waited for the presser to begin. I wasn't sure how I felt about seeing Ben, but I wouldn't let it keep me from my job. At worst, he could gossip about me, but hey, how many people were going to believe I could talk to cats? That reminded me I should stop in and see one of the few people who believed me. Anastasia's shop was just a few blocks away. I'd have to stop in after I was done here.

I felt a hand on my arm and took my nail out of my mouth. Yes, I knew it was a bad habit. No, I couldn't stop it. I looked over and saw Josh from the Tribune as he took the seat next to me.

"Nice work on your story. You set the town on its ear with that one," he said, grinning boyishly.

"Thanks, I appreciate it."

"Did you hear about Dave Freidrich?"

"No, what about him?"

Josh settled into his seat and slid his bag under his chair.

"He got fired! Thirty years with the paper and they let him go."

"No way! Was it over the lies he printed in his story about this case?"

"That, and he got caught breaking the car windows of other reporters. He was found in our parking lot at the Trib. The security camera got him dead to rights."

"No way! My car window got busted out last week. I never knew who did it! I wonder if he's the one who came by my place and pounded on my door, too."

"Could be. I guess he kind of lost it."

"Poor guy, I feel terrible for him. It has to be tough to do one thing your whole life and have it taken from you."

Josh looked at me strangely for a second and then shrugged.

"You're a better person than I am. If he'd broken out my window, I'd make sure he at least paid for it."

"Well, it sounds like he's paid enough. So, any luck on that story you were doing on Ben Walsh?" I asked, not sure I wanted to know the truth.

"Yeah, I found some things. Apparently, there was an internal affairs investigation that went down inside the department right before he quit. It's all hush-hush. I'm still digging."

Huh, that didn't sound good. I looked up as the room hushed and saw Ben walking up to the podium. Dang it, why did he have to look so good after breaking my heart?

"Thanks for coming today, ladies and gentlemen. This is the wrap-up of our case on the death of Mark Brown. I'll take your questions," Ben said, glancing out over the crowd.

His eyes came to a halt when they met mine, and he flushed. He cleared his throat and focused on the question a television reporter was shouting at him.

"Have you captured Gerald Harms yet?"

"No, we're still looking for him. He left town with his wife shortly after Ms. Peters was apprehended."

Ouch, that must have hurt Jordan. I told her he wouldn't leave his wife. As it was, it looked like she was left holding the bag.

"How do you feel about the involvement of the press in capturing the other two suspects in this case?" Josh asked, with an apologetic shrug for me as I whipped around to look at him.

Ben cleared his throat again before answering.

"Ms. Murphy was very beneficial in helping to solve this case, and we appreciate her help."

Huh, not the answer I was expecting. More questions swirled around the room, and I tried to stay focused. I needed to wrap this story up so I could focus on my next one. I'd been given a lead on the mayor hiding a juicy secret, and I couldn't wait to get started on it.

Ben ended the presser amid groans from the other reporters, and we all straggled out into the hall. I rushed to avoid talking to Josh and was surprised when I felt a warm hand on my arm.

"Hannah, wait."

I bit my lip and took a deep breath at the sound of Ben's voice. I wasn't sure my heart could take much interacting with him right now.

"What do you want?"

I didn't care if I sounded rude. Ok, maybe I cared a little.

"I wanted to apologize," Ben said, looking around. "This isn't the place to do it, though. Would you like to have dinner tonight?"

I looked at him, focusing on those light green eyes that haunted my dreams lately. All I could see was the way he looked at me as he told me I was crazy. Yeah, I knew he didn't say precisely that, but it's what I heard.

"I don't know. Not tonight, though. Maybe some other time."

He smiled, and his traitorous dimple winked at me. That stupid dimple.

"Think about it, that's all I'm asking. I'd like to talk with you."

"Ok, I'll let you know."

My heart fluttered a little as I walked out into the sunshine, and there might have been a little extra bounce in my step as I walked to my Blazer. What can I say? I was a sucker for a pair of light green eyes and dimples. Maybe it would all work out.

I drove the few blocks to Anastasia's shop and sat in the parking lot for a few minutes, getting my thoughts in order. I wasn't sure what I wanted to say to her, but I felt pulled to the store. I grabbed my bag and walked in, breathing in the incense as I entered.

"I'll be right there, Hannah."

Weird, how did she know it was me? She must have had a security camera or something. I looked around, trying to spot one, but I came up empty. The soft sound of tinkling bells let me know Anastasia was coming.

Like the last time I'd visited, she was dressed in a flowy skirt and simple top. Her red hair fell down her back in curls, and I briefly wondered how old she was. She had an ageless quality about her.

"It's good to see you again, Anastasia."

"And it's good to see you, Hannah. I'm glad you were successful at your first mission," she said, taking my hand briefly. "Come, we'll have tea."

I followed her to the back, where I found a steaming teapot and two mugs. I knew better than to ask how she knew I was coming. At least this time, when she touched me, she didn't have a look of pain on her face.

"Is this more of your third-eye tea?"

"No, not this time. This is another special blend, for fortitude."

I'd need to look that one up when I got home, but it sure smelled good. I took an appreciative sniff of the mug after she handed it to me.

"So, I guess you know why I'm here?"

"I do, but it's always nice to hear it firsthand."

I told her about the case and everything that happened, including Ben's reaction to my gift. She listened and nodded.

"You've done very well. The spirits are pleased. They'll have another task for you soon."

Yay? I mean, yay! I think. I tried to look happy, but I don't think I was fooling Anastasia. I tried to find the right way to respond to that.

"I'll be interested to see what's in store."

"I think you will be very interested. This next mission will test your newfound abilities and potentially reveal new ones."

"New abilities?"

"All will be revealed at the perfect time, my dear. I can say that the truth will be buried deeply, and it will be up to you to bring it to light. Many lives could be impacted by what you discover."

"So, no pressure, right?"

She laughed softly as we finished our tea. I wanted to make small talk, but I wasn't sure where to start. Hear any good jokes from the spirit world lately? Did spirits joke? Did they ever not speak in riddles? It's a mystery.

She stood and motioned for me to follow.

"I have something for you I think will help. It's a unique object. It's been waiting for you."

That wasn't remotely creepy, right? Anyone? I followed her to the front desk and watched as she slipped a small, ornate box onto the counter. It was made of light-colored wood, with intricate carvings along every inch.

"Wow, this is beautiful. I don't know if I can accept something this nice," I said, reaching for my wallet. "Let me pay you for it."

"No, there is no need for money, my dear. The spirits have said this is for you, and so I shall pass it along. Open it."

Have I mentioned I watch a lot of bad horror movies? Was I about to unleash a mini Pandora's box situation on an unsuspecting populace?

I carefully opened the box and revealed a beautiful rose gold pendant. It was circular, and somehow, a multicolored stone was suspended in the center. I held it up to the light and tried to see if there were tiny wires supporting the stone. I couldn't see any. Weird.

"It's a fire opal. You should research what that stone can do. This one is ancient."

"Oh my, thank you. But it's got to be priceless. The work is incredible. I don't know how they suspended the stone, but this is amazing."

She laughed softly again.

"I feel this will be very important to you. Take it and put it on. Keep it on you at all times."

I slid the necklace over my head and felt the metal against my chest. I expected it to feel cold, but it felt warm and somehow welcoming. I know it sounds a little woo-woo, but it felt like the necklace had come home.

"Oh," I said, unable to come up with anything else.

"Please come visit me again if you have questions. You'll be called upon for your help soon, I think. Be ready."

She walked me to the door, and I traced my steps back to my Blazer in a daze. I collected my thoughts before I pulled out into traffic, ready to head home to Razzy. I couldn't help but feel a bubble of positivity work its way up from my heart. I had a new story to chase, there was hope for Ben and me, and new adventures with Razzy were in store. I couldn't wait.

A NOTE FROM COURTNEY

Thank you for taking the time to read this novel. If you enjoyed the book, please take a few minutes to leave a review. As an independent author, I appreciate the help!

If you'd like to be first in line to hear about new books as they are released, don't forget to sign up for my newsletter. Click here to sign up! https://bit.ly/2H8BSef

COMING SOON... THE TROUBLE AT CITY HALL: A RAZZY CAT COZY MYSTERY

Hannah's got a new story but she never expected a tale of corruption in local politics would turn into a murder.

Now, she's got to work with Razzy to solve this case before she ends up being the next target.

Want to be the first to know when the latest book is released? Join my mailing list! It's just for new releases and special deals, I'll never spam you.

Click here to sign up!
https://bit.ly/2H8BSef

A LITTLE ABOUT ME

Courtney McFarlin currently lives in the Black Hills of South Dakota with her fiancé and their two cats.

Find out more about her books at:
  www.booksbycourtney.com

Follow Courtney on Social Media:

https://twitter.com/booksbycourtney

https://www.instagram.com/courtneymcfarlin/

https://www.facebook.com/booksbycourtneym

BOOKS BY COURTNEY MCFARLIN

Escape from Reality Cozy Mystery Series

Escape from Danger

Escape from the Past

Escape from Hiding

A Razzy Cat Cozy Mystery Series

The Body in the Park

The Trouble at City Hall

The Crime at the Lake

Made in United States
Troutdale, OR
01/05/2024